CASSANDRA

Book One & Book Two

Sandra Evans & John Evans

~SP~
Studio Publishing

This edition first published in the
United States in 2012 by:

Studio Publishing
4750 Bryant Irvin Road
Suite 808-321
Fort Worth, TX 76132
www.studiopublishing.net

Printed in the United States of America.

In memory of my father, Sandor 'Al' Bruck

~ Sandra Bruck Evans ~

CONTENTS

CASSANDRA

Book One

CONTENTS

CASSANDRA & The Lost City of Troy

Book Two

Acknowledgments

Edward Mendelson - our mentor - Professor of English and Comparative Literature at Columbia University - thank you for your constant encouragement and friendship.

Lisa Lesavoy - thank you for introducing us to Edward and for your friendship and continual enthusiasm.

Kevin Koloff - thank you for your sage counsel and friendship over these many years.

Lilly - Sandy's mother - thank you for your unwavering love and support.

Joseph Campbell - Sandy's professor, friend, and don at Sarah Lawrence College - who introduced her to the magical world of mythology.

And old King Priam bent his head in assent, promised the man his daughter, so on he fought, trusting his life to oaths taken, promises struck...

Homer - The Iliad (c.850 B.C.)

Book One

CASSANDRA

~SP~
Studio Publishing

THE MYTH

Three thousand years ago, in 1136 B.C., Cassandra was the daughter of Priam and Hecuba, King and Queen of the ancient city of Troy. She was reported to have been the most beautiful of their daughters.

Legend has it that the Greek god, Apollo, fell in love with Cassandra and offered her the gift of prophecy in exchange for her love. He sent a snake to whisper in her ear, after which she was able to predict the future.

Cassandra rejected Apollo and chose another for her lover. Apollo, angered, could not take away the gift of prophecy, but cursed her so that no one would ever believe her.

PROLOGUE
(Telenos Island, Greece)

Torchlights flickered against the night sky. Twelve hooded figures made their way down a narrow path that wound along a rocky cliff leading to the sea. Carrying torches, they chanted in low voices as they made their way toward the beach.

Two of the hooded figures, who were carrying a large burlap sack filled with something heavy, paused in order to get a better grip. The procession continued down the path. The faces of the young men could be seen in the flickering light from the torches.

At twenty-one years of age, strikingly handsome, with dark brown hair and brown eyes, Nikos Theopoulos' face registered conflict and deep distress.

"We can't do this," Nikos said to one of the hooded figures standing next to him.

"We took an oath," the hooded figure replied.

"I know, but we can still stop it."

"It's too late now," said the hooded figure.

Nikos, in a strained, hoarse voice, said, "God will punish us for this."

~ Cassandra ~

Chapter One

MOVING DAY

(Crestview, New Jersey)
Five Years Later

The forecast had been for rain. Fortunately, the weatherman had been wrong. It was a glorious summer day, not a cloud in the sky. *A perfect day for moving into our new home,* Maria thought.

Standing in the driveway, Maria Theopoulos, twenty-four years old, slender, with long brown hair and brown eyes, watched as the men unloaded pieces of furniture from the green and white moving van parked in the driveway of the modest, two-story suburban New Jersey house.

"Lady, where does this go?" one of the moving men asked, holding up a brass floor lamp.

"In the living room… next to the sofa," Maria answered.

Playing on the lawn, Cassandra Theopoulos, four years old, a strikingly beautiful child with dark brown hair, chiseled, delicate features and large, expressive brown eyes, seemed to be barely aware of the movers.

Maria turned to look at her daughter, catching her breath at her child's beauty. She noticed a small, bookish-looking little boy standing in the street next to the mailbox.

About six years old, Maria guessed. With light brown hair and blue eyes, which loomed large behind thick, tortoise-rimmed glasses, he stood watching the whole moving procedure, too shy to approach Cassandra.

Cassandra, glancing up, noticed the boy, but ignored him. In contrast, he watched her every move with fascination. *Probably one of the neighborhood kids*, Maria thought, turning her attention back to the movers.

Suddenly, Maria heard Cassandra scream. She turned to see her daughter scramble to her feet and start running up the flagstone path leading to the front door.

"Mommy! Mommy! A snake! A snake!" Cassandra tugged on Maria's hand, pulling her toward the front door.

Opening the screen door, Cassandra ran inside, pulling Maria after her.

"Did it bite you?" Maria asked.

Cassandra put her hand to her left ear. "No, but it touched my ear."

"Does it hurt?"

"No."

"Let me take a look." Maria examined Cassandra's ear. "I don't see anything, honey."

Looking through the screen door, Maria noticed that the little boy who had been standing in the street was no longer there.

At that moment, two moving men, carrying an over-stuffed armchair, walked in through the kitchen door.

"My daughter just saw a snake," Maria said, breathless. "Could you go look, please?"

One of the men walked over to Cassandra. Bending down, he asked in a kindly voice, "A little snake?"

"No," Cassandra shook her head. "A big snake."

"How big?"

"*This* big," Cassandra said, stretching her arms apart as far as they would go.

"I'll go look for it," the moving man said, reassuringly.

Moments later, the moving man returned. "There's nothing out there," he said to Maria.

Cassandra looked at him, skeptical.

"Thank you," Maria said to the moving man. "I forgot to ask what your name is."

"It's Jerry, ma'am."

"Thanks, Jerry. One more thing. Could you have the men bring the stuff labeled 'Cassandra's Room' upstairs so that I can start setting up her room?"

"It's already done, ma'am."

"That's wonderful. Thanks," Maria said.

Supporting herself with one hand on the banister, Cassandra began to climb the stairs to her room, Maria following behind her.

Once inside the room, Cassandra seemed comforted by the sight of the familiar furniture from her bedroom in their former apartment in Astoria.

The movers had piled several cardboard boxes in a corner of the room. Opening one marked 'bedclothes', Maria pulled out a mattress pad, comforter and some pillows, and started putting them on Cassandra's bed. When Maria opened the box marked 'Toys', Cassandra walked over and started rummaging through the box for her favorite doll. Maria then began making the bed, relieved that Cassandra seemed to have temporarily taken her mind off the snake.

Maria's cell phone hummed in the pocket of her jeans. Seeing Nikos' name on the caller I.D., she flipped open the phone.

"I'm so glad you called," she said, stepping out into the hall just outside of Cassandra's room.

"What's the matter?" Nikos asked.

"Cassandra had a scare. She saw a snake."

"A snake? Where?"

"In the front yard. I had one of the movers look for it, but he didn't find anything."

"Is she alright?"

"She seems to be."

"Did you see it?"

"No."

"Did anyone else see it?"

"I don't know. There was a little boy, but I don't know if he saw it or not. When are you coming home?"

"I'll be there in a little while. Tell Cassandra I love her."

"Okay. See you later." Stepping back into the room, Maria slipped her cell phone back into her pocket. "That was Daddy. He said he'll be home soon. He told me to tell you that he loves you." Cassandra, absorbed in her project, nodded absentmindedly.

"Ma'am?" Jerry called to Maria from downstairs.

"I'll be right down," Maria called back to him as she stepped out into the hall. In the dim light, she could see Jerry waiting patiently at the bottom of the stairs, clipboard in hand. Maria walked down the stairs to the ground floor.

"You'll have to sign here," Jerry said, handing the clipboard and pen to Maria. Flipping the switch, Maria turned on the light in the hallway and signed where Jerry had indicated.

"I hope your daughter's feeling better," Jerry said, tearing off a copy and handing it to Maria.

"Thanks, Jerry. You've been a big help." Maria watched as Jerry walked across the lawn and climbed up into the seat behind the wheel in the cab of the truck.

Headlights on against the encroaching darkness, the moving van backed slowly out of the driveway.

Turning on the light switch that illuminated the small porch area outside the front door, Maria slid the latch on the screen door, locking it. Walking into the living room, she turned on the floor lamp next to the sofa. Suddenly, she heard the doorbell chime, followed by a friendly-sounding female voice.

"Hello?" the voice said.

Maria hurried to the front door to see an attractive-looking woman in her late twenties, with blondish-brown hair, wearing jeans and a pale blue cotton t-shirt, standing on the front porch.

"I hope I'm not disturbing you. I'm Dana Petrarkos. Tony's mom. We live two houses down from you. I came to see how your daughter's doing."

Tony's mom? Suddenly Maria remembered the little boy who was standing in the street. "Oh, that must have been your son standing by the curb."

"Yes, that was Tony."

"Please, come in." Sliding the latch, Maria opened the screen door. "I'm Maria. My daughter's Cassandra."

"I can't stay long," Dana said, stepping into the foyer. "I have to put Tony to bed. He insisted that I come over. He said that your daughter had been very upset."

"Yes, she saw a snake."

"A snake?" Dana asked, alarm in her voice.

"Yes. Did your son say anything about it?"

"No. He didn't say a word about a snake, but I'll be sure to ask him when I get home."

"Can I offer you anything?"

"No, I really must be getting home," Dana said, turning to leave, then stopping and looking back at Maria. "Oh, by the way. I'm taking Tony to the beach tomorrow. Would you and Cassandra like to come with us?"

"She loves the beach. I'm sure she'll want to go."

"Great." Pulling a piece of paper from her jeans pocket, Dana handed it to Maria. "Here's my number. You can call me anytime up to eleven."

"Thanks, Dana."

"Oh, I forgot," Dana said. "What's your last name? I would have called first, but I didn't know your name."

Reaching for a pen and an empty envelope lying on the sideboard, Maria wrote down her number and handed the envelope to Dana. "It's Theopoulos. I wrote it on the envelope."

"Talk to you later," Dana said, turning and heading down the path toward the curb.

As Maria watched Dana walk away, she noticed Nikos' car pulling into the driveway. Turning off the engine, Nikos opened the door and got out. Except for a few wrinkles beginning to form on his forehead, he still had the same good looks that he had five years ago. Maria walked over to him and kissed him on the cheek.

"Who was that?" Nikos asked, closing the car door.

"Dana Petrarkos. Tony's mother."

"Who's Tony?"

"The little boy I was telling you about."

"Did he see the snake?"

"I don't know. Dana's going to call me back after she speaks with him."

"How's Cassandra?"

"She's upstairs. I'd better go check on her."

"Go ahead," Nikos said, opening the back door of the car. "I brought some food from the restaurant. Are you hungry?" he asked, grabbing some plastic bags that were resting on the seat.

"Starved," Maria called back to him as she walked into the house and up the stairs to Cassandra's room.

Cassandra, lying on her bed, hugging a teddy bear, seemed to be sleeping.

"Honey, are you asleep?" Maria asked softly, walking over to the bed.

"No," Cassandra answered, opening her eyes.

"Daddy's home. He brought some food from work. Are you hungry?"

"No."

"Okay. Maybe later," Maria said, sitting down on the bed. "Tony's mother stopped by to see how you were doing. He's the little boy you saw this afternoon. Remember?"

"Uh huh."

"They're going to the beach tomorrow and have invited us to go with them."

"The beach?" Cassandra asked, interested.

"Yes. Would you like to go?"

"Yes."

"Great."

Just then Nikos appeared in the doorway. "Hi, sweetheart."

"Hi, Daddy," Cassandra said, sitting up, letting go of her teddy bear and opening her arms to hug her father.

Walking over to the bed, Nikos hugged his daughter. "Mommy tells me you had a big scare today."

"I saw a snake," Cassandra said, looking serious. "Daddy?" she asked, a worried look on her face.

"Yes, sweetheart?"

"Can snakes climb walls?"

"No, honey. They can't."

"Are you sure?"

"I'm sure." Nikos paused. "I checked out front when I came home. I didn't see anything. Do you want me to go out back and take a look?"

"Uh huh."

"Okay. You can watch me from the window." Walking out of the room, Nikos headed downstairs. Opening the back door, he stepped out into the yard.

Standing on tiptoe, her nose pressed against the window screen, Cassandra watched as her father, flashlight in hand, searched for the snake.

"Nothing here, honey," Nikos called up to her, moving to another location.

Maria's cell phone hummed. Seeing Dana's name on the caller I.D., she stepped out into the hall.

Nikos looked up at Cassandra's silhouette in the window. "Nothing here either," he said. "Okay?"

Cassandra nodded. Nikos walked back into the house. Climbing up the stairs to the second floor, he saw Maria waiting for him in the hall outside of Cassandra's room.

"There's nothing there," Nikos said. "It must have been her imagination."

"No, it wasn't," Maria said. "I just spoke with Dana. She said that Tony saw the snake."

~ Cassandra ~

Chapter Two

THE BEACH

There were about fifty people in the rolling surf. A lifeguard sat atop his perch, flirting with some teenage girls. Maria and Dana, sitting on folding beach chairs, watched as Tony and Cassandra played at the water's edge.

"Did your husband ever find the snake?" Dana asked, turning to Maria.

"I don't know. He said he was going to call a gardening service and have them look for it."

"Aside from that, how do you like your new house?"

"I love it! It's such a wonderful change from the cramped little apartment in Astoria."

"Did you always live in Queens?"

"No. We lived there for the past five years. Nikos and I moved there right after we got married. We lived in Greece until then."

Looking back at Tony and Cassandra, Maria noticed a boy, a few years older than Tony, standing near them.

"That's cool," Tony heard a voice say. Looking up, he saw a blond-haired boy, about nine years old, admiring his and Cassandra's sandcastle. Cassandra also looked up, then quickly looked down again, too shy to speak, but unable to hide her smile.

"Thanks," Tony said to the boy, grinning. The boy continued on his way, walking down the beach.

Just then, a huge wave rolled onto the beach, covering their sandcastle. As the wave retreated, there was nothing left of their work.

"Don't worry," Tony said, seeing the dismayed look on Cassandra's face. "This happens all the time." Tony started to get up. "I'm hungry."

"Me, too."

"Let's go."

They made their way back to the blanket where Maria and Dana were sitting.

"Mom, can we get some hot dogs?" Tony asked Dana.

"Sure." Turning to Maria and Cassandra, Dana asked, "How about you guys? Hot dogs?"

"Sounds great," Maria said. Cassandra nodded in agreement.

"Tony and I will get them," Dana said. "You guys stay here." Dana and Tony began making their way across the hot sand to the refreshment stand.

Seeing that Cassandra's skin had begun to take on a pinkish color, Maria reached into her beach bag, searching for the sun block.

Suddenly, hearing a small cry coming from Cassandra, Maria turned to see Cassandra's body rigid, her eyes opened wide, unblinking. Her lips were moving, but no sound escaped from her mouth. Kneeling by her daughter's side, Maria noticed that Cassandra's fists were clenched.

"Honey?" Maria said, panic in her voice. Cassandra did not respond.

A few seconds later, Cassandra blinked. Her whole body seemed to relax. Her fists unclenched. She looked into her mother's eyes.

"Did they save the boy?" Cassandra asked.

Maria, having no idea what her daughter was talking about, asked, "What boy?"

"The boy who was swimming out too far. He got tired and was drowning. I tried to yell out, but no one could hear me. Did they save him?"

Maria turned and looked at the lifeguard stand. The lifeguard was sitting there as he had been before. There was no commotion in the water. There was no change. Everything looked calm and normal, just as it had before Cassandra's episode.

"Honey. Nobody drowned. Nobody," Maria said.

Cassandra looked at Maria disbelievingly. "But I *saw* it! I *saw* it," she insisted.

Trying to comfort Cassandra, Maria said, "Nobody

drowned, honey."

"Mommy, I don't feel so good."

"Do you want to go home?"

"Uh huh."

Beginning to pack up their stuff, Maria was startled by Dana's voice.

"What's the matter?" Dana asked.

Looking up, Maria saw Dana and Tony standing near the blanket, overloaded with hot dogs and sodas.

"Cassandra doesn't feel well. I think she's had too much sun. I'd better take her home."

"Do you want us to come with you?" Dana asked.

"No," Maria replied. "We'll be all right."

"But you don't know the way back."

Dana watched as Maria helped Cassandra to her feet. In spite of the sunburn, Cassandra looked pale. She was having trouble standing. Holding Cassandra by the arm, Maria tried to reach for her beach towel.

Taking the towel from Maria's hand, Dana said, "Here, let me help."

"I don't want to stay, Mom," Tony said, putting down the carton of hot dogs and drinks.

"Okay. Then it's decided," Dana said. "We're leaving with you."

* * *

Pulling into her driveway, Maria noticed a yellow piece of paper stuck to the front door of the house. Pressing the remote clipped to her visor, she opened the door and pulled the car into the garage.

Opening the door to the back seat, Maria gently

touched Cassandra's arm. "Honey, we're home."

Cassandra sleepily opened her eyes. She seemed disoriented.

"We're home," Maria repeated, reassuringly.

Cassandra slowly sat up, and with Maria's help, got out of the car, her legs still wobbly.

"Do you want me to carry you inside?" Maria asked.

"No. I can walk," Cassandra said, taking a step. Her knees buckled. She grabbed onto Maria.

"Come on, honey. Let me carry you inside."

Maria lovingly picked up her daughter. Cassandra's arms around her mother's neck, Maria carried her inside and up the stairs to Cassandra's bedroom. She gently put her down on the bed.

"Do you want some juice or something?"

Cassandra shook her head 'no'. Closing her eyes, she seemed to fall asleep immediately. Covering her daughter with a light blanket, Maria left the room and headed downstairs. As she reached the ground floor, she remembered the yellow note on the front door. Opening the front door, she removed the yellow piece of paper. Maria read aloud to herself: "MOUNT OLYMPUS PEST CONTROL." She looked further and saw that the box indicating 'paid' had been checked off. *Did they find the snake? Maybe I should call. There's no phone number on the receipt, just a P.O. box somewhere in Newark.*

Walking into the kitchen, Maria retrieved the phone book from the cabinet. Placing it on the kitchen table, she started flipping through the pages, looking for Mount Olympus Pest Control. *J... K... M... Mid... Motor...*

Mound. There's no Mount Olympus Pest Control!

Picking up the telephone, Maria dialed Nikos' cell phone.

After waiting a moment, she heard Nikos' voice.

"Hi, honey. What's up?" he asked.

"When are you coming home?"

"Why? What's the matter?"

"Cassandra's not feeling well. We had to come home early from the beach."

"What happened?"

"She had some kind of seizure."

"Seizure?"

"It could have been too much sun."

"How is she now?"

"She's upstairs, sleeping," Maria said. "Should I call a doctor?"

"Wait 'til I get home."

"By the way," Maria continued, "I'm looking at a receipt from an exterminator. It was taped to the front door. It's marked 'paid'."

"Yes. The boss said he would take care of it."

"Did they find the snake?"

"I don't know. Probably. I'll be there in a little while."

"Okay. Bye."

Hanging up the phone, Maria headed up the stairs to Cassandra's room. As Maria entered the room, she was relieved and delighted to see her daughter sitting up in bed, playing with her doll.

"Hi, honey. How are you feeling?"

"Okay," Cassandra said, matter-of-factly, continuing to

play with the doll.

"I just spoke with Daddy. He'll be home in a little while. How about a bath before he gets home?" Maria asked, noticing the sand on the bed and on the floor next to Cassandra's flip-flops.

*   *   *

Making a right turn onto Oak Street, Nikos felt a sense of pride as he approached his new home. *The neighborhood... the trees... the well-groomed lawns.* He pulled into the driveway.

*   *   *

Upstairs, Maria was drying Cassandra's hair with a towel. Cassandra was dressed in a clean pair of shorts and a clean t-shirt.

"Hi, honey. I'm home," Nikos called from downstairs.

"Hi, Daddy!" Cassandra, hair still damp, ran out of the bathroom, down the stairs, and into her father's open arms.

"How's my girl?" Nikos asked. Picking her up, he carried her into the kitchen. Putting her back down, he noticed her arms. "Hey, you've got quite a tan."

Cassandra looked at her arms, then back up at Nikos. "I built a sandcastle," she said, smiling.

"You did?"

"Yeah, with Tony. He showed me how."

"Hi, honey," Maria said, as she walked over to Nikos, giving him a kiss on the cheek.

"She looks great," Nikos commented, indicating Cassandra.

"Yes, she seems to be all better now," Maria said in a

low voice so that Cassandra would not hear her.

"I'm hungry," Cassandra announced.

Maria and Nikos smiled at each other, relieved that Cassandra seemed to be all right.

"I'll get dinner started," Maria said.

"Can I go outside?" Cassandra asked. "I want to go on the swing."

"Sure, honey," Maria said.

Heading for the back door, Cassandra ran out into the yard.

"I'll be right there," Nikos called to Cassandra. Turning to Maria, he said, apologetically, "I forgot to bring some food from work."

"That's okay," Maria assured him. "There's plenty left over from last night. I'll warm it up." Opening the refrigerator door, Maria removed a tray of moussaka. Reaching around her into the fridge, Nikos grabbed a cold can of beer, opened it and took a sip.

"So what happened at the beach?" he asked.

"We were just sitting there," Maria said. "Everything seemed fine." Opening the oven door, Maria carefully slid the tray of moussaka into the oven. "All of a sudden, Cassandra got all stiff. She was staring straight ahead. Her arms got rigid and her fists were clenched. I tried to talk to her, but I don't think she heard me. It only lasted for a few seconds."

Nikos took another sip of his beer.

Maria continued. "When she came out of it... I don't know... it was kind of weird."

"What do you mean... 'weird'?"

"She kept asking me, 'Did they save the boy? Did they save the boy?' When I asked her, 'What boy?' she said, 'the boy who was swimming out too far. He got tired and was drowning.' "

"And?" Nikos asked, staring at Maria.

"Nothing had happened. There was no boy. No one was drowning. Everything was normal."

"Where was your friend?"

"Dana and her son had gone to get some hot dogs."

"What do you think it was?"

"I don't know. Maybe too much sun."

"I'll go check on her." Putting his beer on the counter, Nikos headed for the back door.

Noticing that it was five o'clock, Maria switched on the television. The theme for the local news filled the air. As she retrieved the tray of moussaka from the oven, she heard the news anchor's voice.

"Summer fun turned to tragedy today at the New Jersey State Park Beach, when a nine-year-old Bergen County boy, who had swum out too far, got caught in the rip-tide and drowned. It happened so quickly that the lifeguard could not get to the boy in time. WMGM-TV, News 5 reporter, Lindsey Coleman is on the scene right now. What have you got, Lindsey?"

"Hey, Chuck. I'm here with some eye-witnesses to today's tragedy," Lindsey said, walking on the sand, microphone in hand. He approached a group of teenage boys holding surfboards.

"Nikos!" Maria screamed, nearly dropping the tray of moussaka. "Come here! Quick!"

Nikos hurried back into the house. "What is it?"

"Look," Maria said, pointing to the television, her face pale.

They both stood staring at the television.

The reporter continued. "I'm talking to Joey Wilson. He was surfing with some friends at around 3:30, when the incident occurred." Lindsey turned to the teenager. "Tell us what you saw," he said, pushing his microphone toward the boy's face.

"Well, a bunch of us were sitting on our boards, waiting for a wave, when this kid swims by us and just keeps on going. I thought it was kind of strange because the younger kids usually stay in closer to shore."

"Then what happened?" Lindsey asked.

"We caught a wave and rode it in. By that time, people on the beach were all yelling and pointing out to where the kid had been. We turned and looked, but he was already gone."

Lindsey turned away from the surfer and faced the camera. "That's all we have right now, Chuck."

"Have they found the boy?"

"Not yet. A team of divers is out there right now. I'll let you know as soon as we have anything."

"Thanks, Lindsey," the anchorman said, moving on to the next story.

Maria, pale and trembling, grabbed Nikos' arm. "Oh, God. That's exactly what Cassandra told me. But that was at 11:30 in the morning... four hours before it happened."

Chapter Three

THE BIRTHDAY PARTY
(Ten years later)

Maria listened as the radio announcer commented on what perfect beach weather the area had been experiencing. She thought back to ten years ago and the terrible drowning incident at the beach, grateful that her daughter had had no seizures since then.

"Honey?" Maria called from the kitchen.

"Coming!" Cassandra called back, heading downstairs.

At fourteen years of age, just three weeks shy of fifteen, with long brown hair, chiseled features and a slender figure, Cassandra's beauty was undeniable.

"I'm ready," Cassandra said, entering the kitchen and

picking up a small, gift-wrapped box, which had been resting on the kitchen table.

"Okay, let's go," Maria said, grabbing her keys from the counter.

*　　*　　*

Mylar balloons and ribbons were tied to the front porch of the small suburban home. A sign saying 'Happy Birthday, Tommy!' had been attached to the front door.

"Say hi to Dana for me," Maria said, putting the car in park.

"They're back from England?" Cassandra asked, surprised.

"They got back last night," Maria said. "I talked to Dana this morning. We're getting together tomorrow. She's got her hands full right now helping Tommy's mother with the party."

Opening the door, Cassandra stepped out of the car, the gift-wrapped box in her hand.

"Have a good time, honey. Call me when you're ready to leave."

"Thanks, Mom. See you later," Cassandra said, closing the car door.

Maria watched as Cassandra walked across the lawn, disappearing around the side of the house. Putting the car in gear, Maria pulled away from the curb.

In the back yard, several teenagers wearing t-shirts, jeans and shorts, hovered around a picnic table. The atmosphere was relaxed. They all seemed to know each other well. There was a sudden hush as Cassandra appeared. The boys all turned to look at her. She was stunning in her turquoise-blue tank top and white jeans.

Tommy, the 'birthday boy', was standing slightly apart from the group. Walking over to him, Cassandra handed him the gift-wrapped box.

"This is for you," she said.

"Thanks," Tommy said, shaking the box, trying to determine its contents. "What is it?"

"Open it," Cassandra said.

Tommy ripped the paper off the box, exposing a video game. "Cool."

Cassandra smiled.

Placing the box on a small folding table along with his other gifts, Tommy headed for the picnic table. Cassandra started to follow.

"Hey, kiddo," a voice said from behind her. She turned to see Tony standing there.

"Hey, Tony," Cassandra said, her face lighting up. "I didn't expect to see you here." She looked up at Tony for a moment. "You're taller."

"It's been two years," Tony said, caught off guard by Cassandra's beauty. "You look great!"

Dana had started setting the picnic table with brightly colored plastic plates, forks and spoons.

Just then, Denise, Tommy's mother, in her mid-thirties, with short brown hair, appeared at the back door. "Tommy!"

Tommy turned to look at his mother.

"Do you want your present now or after the cake?"

"Now!" Tommy said, his voice filled with anticipation.

Denise disappeared into the house. Moments later, she

reappeared in the backyard, rolling a candy-apple red ten-speed bicycle onto the lawn. There was a large red bow tied to the handlebars.

"Wow! Mom, you got it! I can't believe it!" Tommy ran over to where Denise was standing, putting his hands on the handlebars. Some of the kids gathered around the bike, admiring it. "I want to ride it," Tommy said.

"What about the cake?" Denise asked.

"C'mon, Mom. Just once around the block. Okay?"

"Alright… but hurry back. We'll be waiting."

While everyone's focus was on Tommy, Tony heard a choking sound coming from behind him.

"Bike!"

Tony turned to see Cassandra, her eyes opened wide, her fists clenched tightly. She was trying to speak.

"Bike!" The word was barely audible. Cassandra's whole body appeared rigid.

"Mom! C'mere, quick," Tony called to Dana. "Something's wrong with Cassandra. Watch her for me."

Tony ran around the side of the house and into the street. Seeing Tommy half a block away, peddling his new bicycle, Tony started running after him. As Tommy picked up speed, Tony ran faster. Finally catching up with him, Tony grabbed the bicycle seat and pulled on it, trying to slow the bike down.

"Hey, man. What do you think you're doing?" Tommy protested, angrily.

"Tommy! Stop!" Tony pleaded.

"Get lost!" Tommy yelled. Standing up on the pedals, he lurched forward with extra power, causing Tony to lose his grip and nearly fall. Tony watched as Tommy rode his bicycle into the intersection.

At that moment, a delivery truck drove into the intersection directly in front of Tommy. Horn blaring, the driver slammed on the brakes. Tires squealed. Unable to stop, Tommy rode headlong into the side of the truck. There was a sickening crunch. Tommy was thrown off his bike and onto the pavement. His bike continued forward, under the truck, to be crushed by the rear wheels.

Climbing out of the cab, the truck driver knelt next to Tommy. "Get some help! Call 911. Hurry!" he said, looking up at Tony.

Tony, seeing a woman standing on her front lawn, yelled to her, "Call 911. We need an ambulance… fast!"

Tony turned and started running back to the house. "Cassandra *knew*! She *knew!*" he said, under his breath.

By now, a small crowd of neighbors and children had gathered around the scene of the accident.

Tommy's mother, Denise, ran up the street, followed by Dana. "Tommy!" Denise screamed, hysterically. "Tommy!" Out of breath from running, she knelt down beside her injured son. His face was covered with blood. "Oh, my God!" she cried.

"I'm sorry, lady. I tried to stop, but he was riding too fast," the truck driver attempted to explain.

Tommy moaned slightly.

Within moments, an ambulance arrived. Two paramedics, springing into action, slid a board under Tommy, carefully moving him onto a stretcher and into the ambulance.

"Can I go with him?" Denise pleaded. "I'm his mother."

"Come on. Let's go," one of the paramedics said, helping her climb into the back of the ambulance.

"I'll lock up the house," Dana called to Denise.

Denise nodded as a paramedic climbed into the back of the ambulance, closing the door behind him. The ambulance pulled away, lights flashing, siren wailing.

* * *

Running back to the house, Dana headed straight for the backyard. Cassandra was sitting on one of the benches by the picnic table, Tony standing next to her. Seeing Dana, Cassandra got to her feet.

Some of the kids, having come back from the scene of the accident, started pointing at Cassandra. "It's her fault," one of the girls said.

"Yeah, I heard her say 'bike'," another girl chimed in.

A few more of the girls started whispering, pointing at Cassandra.

"What's going on?" Dana asked Tony.

"They think Cassandra caused it."

Dana turned to the girls. "What's wrong with you? It was an accident."

"I want to go home," Cassandra said, tears welling up in her eyes.

"Come on, honey. Let's go inside and call your mom," Dana said, gently taking Cassandra by the hand. Together, they walked back into the house.

* * *

Maria was putting away some groceries when the telephone rang. "Hello?"

"Maria, it's Dana. Tommy's just had a terrible accident on his bicycle."

"Oh, my God," Maria said.

"Cassandra's okay, but pretty shaken up. Can you pick her up?"

"I'll be right there."

* * *

As Maria approached Maple Street, she saw two patrol cars with lights flashing, one parked in front of a delivery truck, the other behind it. A police officer holding a clipboard was questioning the driver of the truck, while another officer directed traffic. Yellow tape surrounded the scene. Maria, making a right turn onto Maple Street, pulled up to the curb in front of Tommy's house.

Cassandra, who had been waiting for her mother by the front window, opened the screen door and ran to the car. Opening the passenger door, she quickly got in. Maria could tell that Cassandra had been crying.

"They said I caused it," Cassandra said, starting to cry again.

"Caused what?"

"The accident."

Tony walked over to Maria's side of the car, bending down to speak to Maria through the open window. "Cassandra was in the backyard the whole time. She was nowhere near the accident when it happened."

Dana walked up behind Tony. "I have to take the rest of the kids home," she said to Maria. "I'll call you in a little while."

"Thanks, Dana," Maria said, pulling away from the curb.

*   *   *

Maria's cell phone rang as she and Cassandra walked into the kitchen from the garage. Looking at the caller I.D., she answered, "Hi, Dana."

"I found out why the kids were saying that Cassandra had caused the accident," Dana said.

Maria remained silent.

"They said that she had been acting weird, that she kept saying the word 'bike'... right before the accident happened."

"Thanks, Dana," Maria said, her hands trembling as she ended the call.

Oh, God. It's happening again.

Chapter Four

DR. ZAREN

Dr. Michael Zaren, Chief of Neurology at Crestview Memorial Hospital, in his mid-forties, with light brown hair graying at the temples, looked up after reviewing Cassandra's chart.

"According to the records that Cassandra's pediatrician faxed me, she had a mild seizure when she was four."

"That's correct," Maria said.

"And there's been nothing for the past ten years until last week?"

"That's right," Maria confirmed.

"All I can say is that after having completed my physical

examination, it appears that your daughter is in perfect health."

Maria looked relieved.

"However, just to be on the safe side, I'd like to run an EEG to rule out any potential neurological damage."

"What's an EEG?" Cassandra asked, stepping down off the examining table.

"An electroencephalogram. It's a recording of a person's brain waves." Noticing that Cassandra was looking apprehensive, he added, "Don't worry. It won't hurt. All we're going to do is put a cap on your head. You'll just sit there while we record the information that's coming from your brain. Come with me," he said, opening the door of the examination room.

Dr. Zaren, Maria and Cassandra walked down the hall together, stopping in front of a large heavy metal door, upon which a sign read: ELECTROENCEPHALOG-RAPHY. As the trio entered the room, Dr. Zaren pushed a button on the intercom. "Peggy, would you please come to EEG?"

Within seconds, a friendly-looking, red-haired nurse in her early thirties appeared at the door.

Dr. Zaren gestured for Maria to have a seat in the guest chair. "Peggy, would you please prepare Cassandra for an EEG?"

"Yes, doctor." Peggy moved about the room with an air of experience and professionalism. Reaching into different drawers, she pulled out several small plastic bags containing wires and connectors. "Why don't you sit in that chair over there," she said to Cassandra, gesturing to a reclining chair.

At that moment, a female voice crackled over the intercom, "Dr. Zaren, line three. Dr. Zaren, line three."

Dr. Zaren walked over to the door and opened it. "I'll be right back."

Cassandra sat down in the chair.

Slipping what looked like a spandex bathing cap with connectors on it over Cassandra's head, Peggy tucked in some wisps of hair, adjusting the cap until it fit snugly on Cassandra's head. She then began attaching wires to the connectors on the cap and their opposite ends to their corresponding terminals on the EEG recorder. Before long, there were about thirty wires emanating from the cap on Cassandra's head.

Starting to feel nervous, Maria grabbed the armrests of her chair and took a deep breath.

Turning on the video monitor, Peggy pointed to the screen. "You see those waves moving across the screen?"

"Yes," Cassandra said.

"Those are your brain waves. That's electricity coming from your brain."

"Electricity?" Maria asked, concerned.

"Yes. Everyone's brain gives off electrical impulses. That's how the nervous system works."

Cassandra, becoming more interested, appeared visibly less apprehensive. In contrast, Maria was getting more nervous by the minute.

"Are we ready to go?" Dr. Zaren asked, entering the room and closing the door behind him.

Staring at the electrodes on Cassandra's head, Maria

asked, "All those wires. Is it safe?"

"Completely safe," Dr. Zaren said.

"But what about the electricity?" Maria asked.

"There is more electricity coming from your daughter than is put out by the EEG recorder. She'll be fine."

Dimming the lights in the room, Dr. Zaren switched on the EEG recorder and turned to Cassandra. "Now... I want you to keep your eyes open and look straight ahead."

"What if I blink?"

"That's fine. How are we doing?"

"Okay."

Dr. Zaren looked at the monitor, studying it for a moment. Turning to Maria, he said in a low voice to prevent Cassandra from hearing, "I'm going to attempt to induce a seizure. Would you like to leave the room?"

"No. I'll stay," Maria said, in spite of her growing anxiety. She tightened her grasp on the armrests of her chair.

Turning back to Cassandra, Dr. Zaren said, "I want you to look straight ahead. I'm going to aim a light into your eyes. It's going to start flashing. If you don't feel well, get dizzy, or feel uncomfortable in any way, let me know and I'll stop. Okay?"

"Okay," Cassandra replied.

Dr. Zaren positioned the light and turned it on. As the light flashed in strobe-like fashion, the room began to take on the look of an old science fiction movie. Cassandra, wires emanating from the skin-tight cap covering her head, kept staring at the light, wide-eyed.

"Keep looking straight ahead," he said to Cassandra.

Feeling faint, Maria got up from her chair, opened the

door and stepped out into the hall, closing the door behind her.

A few moments later, the light stopped flashing. Turning on the room light, Dr. Zaren turned to Cassandra and asked, "How are we doing?"

"Fine," Cassandra said, apparently unfazed by the experience.

Disconnecting the wires attached to the cap, Peggy tossed them onto a nearby table. Walking over to the door, she opened it. "Dr. Zaren will be right out," she said to Maria.

Dr. Zaren stepped out into the hall. "The EEG appears to be completely normal," he said to Maria. "If she had any tendency toward petit mal seizure, she would have reacted to the flashing light."

Maria's whole body seemed to relax. "Thank you, doctor."

"You're very welcome," he said to Maria. Standing in the doorway to the EEG room, Dr. Zaren waved to Cassandra. "Bye, dear. You take care now." Cassandra waved back. Dr. Zaren turned and started to walk down the hallway.

"Dr. Zaren?" Maria called out to him.

"Yes?" he said, turning and walking back to where Maria was standing.

"Have you ever heard of people seeing things before they happen?"

"You may have heard of déjà vu. That happens when there is a slight delay in the neural transmission of a visual image to the brain. It can cause people to feel that they are familiar with a place which they have never visited before."

"No. I mean just the opposite. When one sees something happen *before* it happens."

"You mean precognition?" he asked, looking skeptical. "I'm not familiar with any valid studies in that area. Why do you ask?"

"Yesterday, at a birthday party, Cassandra saw an accident before it happened." Maria held her breath.

"I wouldn't be surprised by something like that. Again, it has to do with the transmission of the visual image to the brain. The person sees it, but the brain doesn't register it right away."

"But Cassandra wasn't at the scene when the accident occurred."

"Then it's impossible."

At that point, it became apparent to Maria that the conversation had ended. She watched as Dr. Zaren walked down the hall toward his office.

Chapter Five

THE TRAIN

"So what happened at the doctor's?" Nikos asked, opening the fridge and taking out a can of beer.

"He did a lot of tests," Maria said.

"And?"

"He said that everything was normal."

"That's great. Where is she?"

"Hi, Dad."

Nikos turned to see Cassandra standing in the doorway. Walking over to her father, she gave him a hug.

"Hi, sweetheart," Nikos said, hugging her back.

"You're home early," Cassandra observed.

"I have to go to Philly tomorrow."

Maria looked at Nikos. "You never said anything about Philadelphia."

"Stavros wants me to be there for the opening of the new restaurant," Nikos said, taking a sip from his beer.

"But you just got back from an opening in Chicago," Maria said.

"Look, he's my boss. I've got to be there. Besides, he depends on me."

"When are you going?" Cassandra asked, in an effort to diffuse the tension.

"In the morning. I'm catching the eight-thirty train."

"Why aren't you taking the car?" Maria asked. "It's not that far."

"I have a lot of work to do. I'll be able to get it done on the train." Leaving his beer on the counter, Nikos picked up his briefcase and headed for the den. Once at his desk, he opened his briefcase and removed the train schedule. Taking a pen from his shirt pocket, he circled the departure time and tossed the schedule onto his desk. "I'll be out back," he called to Maria and headed for the back door.

* * *

"Mom, can I use Dad's computer?" Cassandra called from upstairs. "Mine just crashed."

"Sure," Maria answered.

Walking downstairs and into the den, Cassandra went over to the computer. Noticing the train schedule lying on the desk, she reached over and picked it up.

Suddenly, Cassandra's body stiffened. Her fists clenched. Her eyes were opened wide, unblinking. After a few seconds, her body relaxed and her fists unclenched. She blinked a few times, momentarily disoriented.

"Daddy!" she screamed, panic in her voice. Running out of the den, she headed for the back door, out into the yard, and over to where Nikos was standing.

"Daddy!" she said, breathless.

"What's the matter?"

"Don't go!"

"What are you talking about?"

"The train!"

"What about the train?" Nikos asked, staring at Cassandra.

"It's going to crash."

"How do you know?"

"I saw it."

"Nothing's going to happen. I'm taking the train."

Hysterical, Cassandra ran back into the house, and headed for the kitchen. "Mom, don't let Dad take the train."

"What's going on?" Maria asked, as Nikos entered the kitchen.

"Cassandra doesn't want me to take the train. She says it's going to crash."

"Did she see it?"

"See what?"

"The crash."

"She says she did," Nikos said.

"Then you'd better not go."

"What? You, too?" Nikos asked, staring at Maria.

"Don't go, Nikos," Maria warned.

"I can't believe this. I'm taking the train and that's the end of it." Nikos turned and stormed out of the kitchen.

"Don't let him go, Mom."

"I'll talk to him."

Sensing an argument coming, Cassandra walked out of the house and into the backyard. The leaves in the trees began to rustle as the wind picked up.

"Cassandra," a mysterious voice called to her in the wind.

"Daddy?" Cassandra turned around, but saw nothing. She heard the strange voice again. "Cassandra."

Frightened, Cassandra ran back into the house and locked the door behind her.

* * *

Standing in the doorway to the bedroom, Maria watched as Nikos closed his suitcase, putting it on the floor next to his nightstand.

"Nikos…," Maria started to say.

"I don't want to talk about it. I'm going, and that's that. I'll be downstairs. I have a lot of work to do."

Maria stepped aside as Nikos walked past her and into the hall.

* * *

The morning sun was streaming in through the window in Cassandra's room. Looking in, Maria saw that Cassandra was awake.

"Daddy called earlier. You were sleeping, so I didn't wake you. He said he's not taking the train."

"He's not?" Cassandra asked, sitting up. "What happened?"

"He said they're working on the tracks and his train is going to be delayed. He didn't want to wait, so he's taking the car."

* * *

Sitting at her father's desk, Cassandra looked at the monitor of Nikos' computer. As she started to write something down on a piece of paper, her pen ran out of ink. Looking around for another pen and not seeing one, she opened the desk drawer. In the drawer, she noticed a small red velvet jewelry box. Removing the box from the drawer, she opened it to find a strange-looking gold ring, with distinctive markings on an onyx stone. Taking the ring from the box, Cassandra got up and headed for the kitchen.

"Mom? What's this?" Cassandra asked, holding the ring up for Maria to see.

Drying her hands on a dishtowel, Maria took the ring and examined it.

"I have no idea. I've never seen it before. Where'd you find it?"

"In Dad's desk drawer."

"You'd better put it back," Maria said, handing the ring back to her daughter. Cassandra took the ring and headed for the den.

Maria glanced at the clock on the kitchen wall. *9:45.* She turned on the radio. Popular music filled the air.

Returning to the kitchen, Cassandra headed for the refrigerator, opened the door and retrieved a carton of orange juice. The music on the radio was suddenly interrupted by the voice of the announcer.

"WNJY-FM, Breaking News. This just in off the wire. A New Jersey Transit commuter train bound for Philadelphia collided with an oncoming train about forty miles east of Philadelphia at nine-twenty this morning."

Maria and Cassandra looked at each other. Closing the refrigerator door, Cassandra put the carton of orange juice on the counter.

"Authorities are reporting that a large number of passengers have been injured. Many are feared dead." The announcer continued, "A New Jersey Transit spokesperson said that the Philadelphia bound train ended up on the wrong track when it was routed around some repairs that were being done. Now back to our regular programming."

Picking up the remote, Cassandra turned on the television. Maria turned off the radio. The two of them stood, frozen in place, staring at the television.

Images of mangled passenger cars, ambulances and paramedics carrying injured passengers on stretchers, filled the screen.

"In case you've just tuned in, we're looking at images of the horrific train wreck that occurred about half an hour ago," the news anchor said. "Heather Markson of WPHI, our Philadelphia affiliate, is on the scene. What have you got for us, Heather?"

Holding a microphone in her hand, standing in an area alongside the train wreckage, Heather Markson looked at the camera.

"Well, Sean, it's hard to describe the devastation. The Philadelphia bound passenger train was traveling at top speed when it collided head-on with a New York bound freight train." She paused for a moment. "I haven't been given a definitive number yet, but I've heard that there could be as many as thirty fatalities."

The telephone rang loudly, startling Maria and Cassandra. Maria reached for the receiver.

"Hello?"

"Hi, honey," Nikos said.

Covering the mouthpiece, Maria whispered to Cassandra, "It's Daddy."

Cassandra quickly turned off the television. Removing her hand from the mouthpiece, Maria asked, "Where are you?"

"I'm in Philly. I just checked into the hotel."

"Did you hear about the accident?"

"What accident?"

"The train that you were supposed to be on… it collided with another train."

Nikos was silent for a moment. "Where's Cassandra?" he asked.

"She's right here."

"Is she okay?"

"Yes. She's fine."

"Look, I've got to go to my meeting. I'll call you tonight"

"Okay. Bye," Maria said, hanging up the phone. She stood thinking for a moment, then dialed information.

"Who are you calling?" Cassandra asked.

"Information." Maria listened to the operator, then said, "Crestview… the Greek Orthodox Church."

Cassandra watched as Maria wrote down the number.

Chapter Six

FATHER GEORGE

Maria and Cassandra climbed the front steps of St. Sophia's Greek Orthodox Cathedral, entering through the heavy, open, wooden door. Walking down the center aisle, they sat down in one of the wooden pews. As she looked around the church, Maria was surprised to see so few people.

A young man in his early thirties, wearing a white shirt, tie, and casual slacks, approached them.

"Mrs. Theopoulos?" he asked.

"Yes?"

"I'm Peter... Father George's secretary. Father George

can see you now."

Maria and Cassandra stood up and stepped into the aisle.

"Please come with me," Peter said.

*　*　*

Father George, in his early fifties, with graying hair, a friendly face and intelligent eyes, sat behind his desk.

"Come in," he said, getting up from his chair.

Maria and Cassandra entered the office, Maria bowing her head slightly.

"Hello, Father. Thank you for seeing us."

Walking around his desk, Father George extended his right hand to Maria.

"My pleasure," he said, shaking Maria's hand. "And you must be Cassandra."

Cassandra nodded, smiling shyly.

"Please, have a seat," he said, gesturing to the two chairs facing his desk. He walked back to his chair and sat down. Turning to Maria, he said, "Peter mentioned that you had a matter of some urgency that you wanted to discuss with me."

There was a knock at the door.

"Yes?" Father George asked.

Opening the door, Peter entered the room. "Mrs. Dimitriou is on the phone," Peter said, handing Father George a piece of paper.

Putting on his reading glasses, Father George glanced at the note, then turned to Maria. "Excuse me. I have to take this call. It'll just be a moment," he said, picking up the phone. "Yes, Janet. It's Father George. I need to know what hospital he's in." He listened a moment. "Okay. Just give Peter the information and tell them that I'll be there." Father George put the caller on hold and looked up at Peter. "Please get the information regarding the hospital from Mrs. Dimitriou."

"Yes, Father," Peter said, walking out of the room, closing the door behind him.

Father George turned back to Maria. "I'm sorry," he said. "There's been a terrible railroad accident."

"I know about the accident," Maria said. "That's why we're here."

"Was someone in your family on that train?"

"My husband was supposed to be, but Cassandra begged him not to go."

"Why did you do that?" Father George asked, turning to Cassandra.

"I knew it was going to crash."

Father George peered at Cassandra over the top of his reading glasses. "How did you know?"

Cassandra looked at her mother, then back at Father George.

"I saw it."

Father George was silent for a moment, then turned to Maria. "Could it be a coincidence?"

"No."

"How can you be so sure?" he asked.

"Because it's not the first time," Maria said.

"What do you mean... not the first time?"

"It's not the first time that Cassandra has seen something before it happened."

Hearing her cell phone ring, Maria removed it from her pocketbook, looked at the caller I.D., and turned off the ringer.

"Do you have to take that call?" Father George asked.

"No. It's my husband. He'd be furious if he knew that we were in church." Putting the phone back in her bag, Maria said, "I'll explain later."

Father George nodded. "You were telling me," he said, taking off his reading glasses.

"The first time it happened was when she was four. She saw a little boy drowning at the beach… four hours before it happened."

Father George looked at Cassandra for a moment.

Maria continued, "There was nothing for ten years. Now it's happening again. It started three days ago, at a friend's birthday party."

"What happened?" Father George asked.

"Cassandra saw her friend have an accident on his bicycle about three minutes before it happened."

Father George remained quiet for a moment, then asked Maria, "How is the boy now?"

"He has a few broken bones, but the doctors say that he'll be okay."

"So nothing after the drowning incident until the other day?"

"That's right. And then today… the train accident." Maria paused a moment, then said, "I took her to a neurologist because she seemed to have some kind of seizure during each episode, but the doctor found nothing wrong with her."

Father George turned to Cassandra. "Tell me, my dear. What does it feel like when you're seeing these things happen?"

"Well, first I start to feel kind of strange. It's almost like I'm going to black out or something." Cassandra continued, "Then I see it happening… like I'm right there. I try to yell out."

"Does anyone hear you?" Father George asked.

"Yes. Some of the kids heard me. That's why they thought I caused the accident." Cassandra thought back. "Tony heard me and believed me. He tried to stop the bike."

"Who's Tony?"

"My best friend. He and his parents just got back from England. They were there for two years."

Maria interjected, "The police report said that a neighbor who had witnessed the accident saw Tony trying to slow the bicycle down by grabbing onto the seat. The report also said that the truck driver was certain that Tony's slowing the bike down, even for those few seconds, prevented the boy from being killed."

Father George leaned back in his chair, thinking. "So Cassandra's warning saved the boy's life." The room was quiet.

"Father George?" Cassandra asked, breaking the silence.

"Yes, Cassandra?"

"Do you know anyone else who's like me?"

"Well, there were the prophets of Biblical times. But, I personally have never known anyone with the gift of prophecy." He paused. "However, I've known some people who have had things happen to them that were difficult to explain."

"Like what?" Cassandra asked.

"Sometimes a spirit can inhabit a person's body and soul, causing them to do things that they normally could not, like speaking in a foreign language that the person never learned, or performing physical acts beyond the person's normal strength, or hearing voices telling them to do strange things."

Cassandra thought back to the strange voice she heard calling her name in the backyard. "Really?"

"Yes. I've seen it with my own eyes."

"Were you able to help them?" Cassandra asked.

"Some of them," Father George said. "There are prayers that can help free the soul that's trapped inside the person."

"Does it hurt?" Cassandra asked, apprehensive.

"The prayers don't hurt, but sometimes there can be a struggle when the spirit doesn't want to leave." He paused a moment. "I have a prayer that I'd like to try right now. Are you okay with that?"

Cassandra looked at Maria, then back at Father George.

"I guess so," she said, tentatively.

Getting up from his chair, Father George walked over to Cassandra. "I need for you to stand up."

Cassandra got up from her chair. Placing his right hand on her forehead, Father George began to pray, almost inaudibly. He was completely focused on Cassandra. After a moment, he removed his hand.

"Something's blocking me," he said, stepping back for a moment. Suddenly, Cassandra began gasping for air. Maria stood up and started to move toward her. Father George motioned for Maria to stop.

"Let her be," he said.

Cassandra continued to gasp for air, coughing, clutching at her throat.

"Oh, God," Maria said. "Father George, please help her."

Father George placed his hand on Cassandra's forehead and said, "God, the Father, Creator of heaven and earth, protect this child."

Within seconds, Cassandra's breathing returned to normal. Father George helped her back into her chair. Walking back to his chair, he sat down. After waiting for a moment, he asked, "Can you tell me what happened? What did you see?"

"I was on a beach at the ocean. It was dark. I heard chanting."

Father George listened attentively. "Go on."

"Then I felt myself sinking into the wet sand. The waves started coming in. Closer and closer... higher and higher. Then the water was over my head. I couldn't breathe." Cassandra paused for a moment, then asked, "Did you get rid of it?"

"Get rid of what?" Father George asked.

"The bad spirit."

"There was no bad spirit. I felt some kind of resistance... as if there were something trying to block my communication with you." Getting up from his chair, Father George said, "We should try it again sometime. There's definitely something there. I'm sure that you'd feel better if you were freed of whatever it is." He walked around his desk. "I'm afraid I'm going to have to end our session now. I have to leave for the hospital."

Maria and Cassandra got up from their chairs. The three of them walked toward the door. Turning to Father George, Maria, almost in a whisper, asked, "Why are these things happening?"

Father George and Maria stopped and stood in the hall while Cassandra continued walking toward the church entrance.

"Did anything like what she just described ever happen to Cassandra?"

"No, never. She loves the water."

Turning around, Cassandra looked at Maria, questioningly.

"Go ahead, honey," Maria said. "I'll be right there. I just want to speak with Father George for a moment."

Cassandra continued walking toward the entrance.

"No one can know exactly why these things happen," Father George continued. "There is usually some connection between the person and the spirit, be it through family or a close acquaintance."

Maria started to get emotional. "We may not have kept up our religion, Father, but Nikos and I are good people."

"Cassandra's problem probably has no connection with you or your husband. She's such an intelligent young lady with a true willingness to cooperate. I feel that the likelihood of her getting better is good." Father George paused, thinking for a moment. "Maria?"

"Yes, Father?"

"You mentioned that your husband would be furious if he knew that you and Cassandra were in church. Why is that?"

"It wasn't always that way," Maria explained. "I come from a very religious family. When Nikos and I were young, our families went to church together."

"Mom?" Cassandra called from down the hall.

"I'm coming, honey."

*   *   *

Pulling into the driveway, Maria pressed the remote, opening the garage door.

"Uh oh. Daddy's home," Maria said, tensing up.

Cassandra looked up to see her father's car parked in the garage. "Do you think he knows?"

"We'll soon find out."

Maria and Cassandra entered the kitchen to see Nikos leaning against the kitchen counter, his arms folded across his chest, a crumpled, empty beer can lying on the counter next to him.

"Hi, honey. You're home early," Maria said, trying to act nonchalant.

"Hi, Daddy," Cassandra said, meekly.

"You'd better go upstairs," Nikos said to Cassandra. "I have to talk to your mother."

Cassandra looked at Maria.

"It's okay, honey. Go ahead," Maria said.

Reluctantly, Cassandra left the kitchen and started

climbing the stairs to the second floor. She stopped halfway up the stairs, trying to listen.

"I saw your car in the parking lot of St. Sophia's. What the hell were you doing there?" Nikos asked.

Maria remained silent.

"I called you on your cell phone. Why didn't you answer?"

"It must've been turned off," Maria replied.

"Nice. How am I supposed to reach you if you turn your phone off?"

"I'm sorry."

"So what were you and Cassandra doing at St. Sophia's?"

"We were talking to a priest."

"Why in the world would you be going to see a priest?"

"To see if he could help Cassandra."

"You told me that Dr. Zaren said that there was nothing wrong with her, right?"

"Yes," Maria said, timidly.

"Then why did you go to see a priest?"

Maria looked down.

"How long have you been seeing him?"

"Today was the first time."

"And it'd better be the last. Do you understand?" Nikos said, his voice filled with anger. "Look at me when I'm talking to you!" he commanded.

Maria looked up.

"The next time she has a seizure, you're going to take her to a new doctor. Stavros gave me the name of a specialist."

Cassandra, frightened, ran up the stairs and into her room, closing the door behind her.

~ Cassandra ~

Chapter Seven

THE MOVIE

Cassandra read aloud from the computer on Nikos' desk. "**[pree-kog-nish-uhn]** -noun: Knowledge of an event prior to its occurrence."

Hearing Cassandra's voice coming from the den, Maria walked into the room. "What are you doing, honey?" she asked.

"Looking up a word."

"What word?"

"Precognition."

"Where did you learn that?"

"Dr. Zaren mentioned it when you were talking with

him in the hall."

"How much of our conversation did you hear?"

"Most of it." Cassandra paused, then looked up at her mother. "It's what I have, isn't it, Mom?"

"Yes."

"Then why did Dr. Zaren say it's not possible?"

"I don't know, honey."

"If it's not possible, why is it in the dictionary?"

Hearing the phone ring, Maria picked up the receiver. "She's right here," Maria said, handing the phone to Cassandra. "It's Tiffany."

"Hey, Tiff. What's up?" Cassandra listened for a moment. "Hold on. I'll ask." Looking up at Maria, Cassandra asked, "Can I go to the movies with Tiffany and Cindy?"

"When?"

"This afternoon."

"Sure."

"Tiffany's mom is taking us there. Can you pick us up?"

"Of course. What time?"

"I'm not sure." Cassandra spoke into the phone. "She said that she can pick us up." Cassandra listened for a few seconds. "Okay. See ya'. Bye," she said, hanging up the phone.

"What's playing?" Maria asked.

"E.T."

"Didn't you already see it?"

"Yes. When I was little, but I want to see it again."

Maria reached for the newspaper on Nikos' desk. Opening it to the entertainment section, she located the ad for the movie and tore it out of the paper. "It's at the Majestic. It ends just before five," she said, putting the torn piece of newspaper down on the desk.

Picking up the ad, Cassandra asked, "Can I have this?"

"Sure."

"I'd better get ready," Cassandra said, closing the browser on the computer. Getting up from the chair, she left the den and headed upstairs.

*   *   *

"Hi, honey," Nikos said, walking into the kitchen from the garage.

"You're home early," Maria commented.

"I have to catch a three o'clock plane for Cincinnati."

"Cincinnati?"

"Why are you looking at me like that?" Nikos asked, annoyed.

"Aren't you ever going to spend some time at home?"

"Don't start with me, Maria. We've been through this before."

*   *   *

Standing by her desk, Cassandra could hear her parents arguing. In her hand, she held the torn piece of newspaper with the "E.T." ad on it. Suddenly, her body stiffened. Her fists clenched. Her eyes were opened wide, unblinking. In her mind's eye, she saw a movie screen. It was late at night. A woman woke up and went into her little boy's room. He was not there. The woman was frightened. Running outside, she looked for him, but couldn't find him anywhere.

At that moment, there was a loud explosion in the theatre. Thick smoke was everywhere. Everyone was pushing and screaming, trying to get out of the theatre, but the exit doors were jammed. No one could get out. People began to scream even louder.

Cassandra snapped back to the present. Looking down at the scrap of newspaper on her desk, she felt a sense of relief. *We're going to see E.T. I don't remember any scene about a missing little boy*, she thought to herself. Slightly relieved, but still unsettled, she wanted to tell her mother about what had just happened. Leaving her room, she started to go downstairs.

In the kitchen, the argument between her parents had escalated to near shouting. Stopping halfway down the stairs, Cassandra heard her mother's voice.

"What makes you think that this new doctor will be better than Dr. Zaren?"

Cassandra froze in place on the stairway, listening.

"Stavros said so."

"Stavros? What makes him an expert on what's best for our daughter? What's wrong with Dr. Zaren anyway?"

Grabbing onto the banister, Cassandra held her breath.

"He's the best doctor in the whole county," Maria continued. "And Cassandra likes him. Why send her to somebody else? Besides, she doesn't need a doctor."

"If Cassandra has another seizure, you're taking her to see this new doctor. He's a specialist."

Turning around, Cassandra ran up the stairs to her room. She sat down at her desk and started writing on a notepad.

A car horn honked twice. "They're here," Maria called

up from the kitchen.

"Coming!" Cassandra called back. Tearing the page from the pad, she folded the note and tucked it into her jeans pocket. Getting up from her desk, she headed downstairs.

"How about a goodbye hug?" Nikos asked, standing at the base of the stairs.

"Bye, Dad," Cassandra said, giving him a half-hearted hug.

"Have a good time, sweetheart," he said. "I'll see you Monday night."

"Don't forget to take some money," Maria said, handing Cassandra a twenty-dollar bill.

Opening the screen door, Cassandra stepped outside onto the porch. "Mom?"

"Yes, honey?"

"I have something for you." Pulling the folded piece of paper from her jeans pocket, Cassandra slipped it into Maria's pocket.

"What is it?"

"A note, but don't read it until after Daddy leaves," Cassandra said, turning and running toward the car waiting at the curb.

Waving to Tiffany's mother, Maria called out to her, "I'll pick them up at quarter of."

Opening the backseat passenger door, Cassandra got in.

"Bye, Mom," she said, pulling the door shut.

"Bye, honey." Maria watched as the car pulled away. She touched the note in her pocket. *I wonder what it's about.*

I bet she heard us arguing. Closing the screen door, Maria headed toward the kitchen, where Nikos was sitting at the table, sipping a cup of coffee.

* * *

Several disgruntled-looking teenagers were milling around on the sidewalk in front of the Majestic Theater, some of them walking away. Arriving at the ticket booth, it became apparent to Cassandra, Tiffany and Cindy why the kids were angry. The movie had been changed. Instead of "E.T.", they were playing "Close Encounters of the Third Kind."

"Do you want to leave or do you want to see it?" Cindy asked.

"Let's see it," Tiffany said. "I heard that it's really good."

Buying their tickets, the girls went into the lobby of the theatre, which was full of kids lined up to buy popcorn and soda. Cassandra, Tiffany and Cindy made their way into the theatre, managing to find three good seats even though the house was already pretty full. The lights dimmed. The movie began.

* * *

Taking one last sip of his coffee, Nikos put the cup down on the saucer. "Gotta' run," he said, getting up from his chair and heading for the door to the garage. "I'll see you Monday night."

Maria listened as the garage door opened. She heard Nikos start his car and back out of the garage.

* * *

As Cassandra watched the movie, she began to grow uneasy. The scene that she had seen in her mind was beginning to play out on the screen in front of her. It was the middle of the night. A woman woke up and went into her little boy's room. The boy wasn't there.

Cassandra leaned over to Tiffany. "I think we'd better leave," she whispered.

"What for?"

"I have a feeling that something bad is going to happen,"

"It's only a movie, Cassandra."

"No, I mean here… in the theatre."

"Shhh!!!" The people sitting in the row behind Cassandra were starting to get annoyed.

*   *   *

Reaching into her jeans pocket, Maria removed Cassandra's note. Unfolding it, she began to read:

Dear Mom,

I don't want you to worry, but I think I had another one of my 'things'. I wanted to tell you about it, but I was afraid to because Daddy said he would make me go to that new doctor.

Okay, here's what I saw:

At the movie, it wasn't E.T. In the movie, it was late at night. A woman woke up and went into her little boy's room. He was gone.

Beginning to feel a knot start to tighten in her stomach, Maria read on:

She looked everywhere for him. She was scared. She even ran outside, looking for him. She couldn't find him. Then there was a big explosion in the theater. People tried to get out, but they couldn't.

I tried to warn them, but they wouldn't listen to me.

But don't worry, we're going to see E.T. and what I saw was not in the movie.

Just in case, please keep your cell phone turned on. Okay?

I love you,
Cassandra

Remembering that Cassandra had asked for the ad for the movie, Maria ran quickly up the stairs to Cassandra's room. Seeing the ad on Cassandra's desk, she picked it up and dialed the number of the theater on her cell phone.

On the other end of the line, Maria heard, "Majestic Theatre."

"Can you tell me when E.T. lets out?"

"E.T.'s not playing."

"Why not?" Maria asked, feeling the knot in her stomach grow tighter.

"There was an issue with one of the reels. They're showing Close Encounters instead."

"Thank you," Maria mumbled, her mind racing. She thought back to when she and Nikos had seen Close Encounters. Suddenly, she remembered the scene near the beginning of the movie, where the little boy disappeared and his mother couldn't find him anywhere… exactly as Cassandra had described it.

Oh, my God. Running down the stairs and into the kitchen, she grabbed her keys from the counter and headed for the garage.

*   *   *

"We've got to get out of here," Cassandra whispered, tugging on Tiffany's arm.

"What's wrong with you?" Tiffany asked. "Let go of me!" she said, pulling her arm away from Cassandra.

"Shut up in front!" an angry moviegoer shouted.

Cassandra glanced up at the movie screen. She saw the woman in the movie starting to panic. The woman was looking everywhere for her little boy. She went outside to look for him, but he was gone.

It's the same scene, Cassandra thought to herself. "Come on! Let's go!" she said to Tiffany and Cindy, panic in her voice.

At that moment, the theatre manager appeared next to Cassandra's seat, shining his flashlight in her face. "Miss, if you're not going to be quiet," he said, "you're going to have to leave."

"Tiffany… Cindy… we've got to get out of here," Cassandra insisted.

"You're crazy. Leave us alone," Tiffany said, angrily.

Taking Cassandra firmly by the arm, the theatre manager said, "Come with me, miss," then escorted her to the back of the theatre and into the lobby.

"Please, mister. You've got to tell people to get out of here. Something terrible is going to happen." Cassandra looked helplessly at the manager. "Pleeease!" Starting to cry, she ran out the front door of the theater and down the sidewalk.

Pulling up to the curb in front of the theater, Maria got out of her car and ran to the ticket booth.

"You can't leave your car there," the ticket taker admonished Maria.

"Have you seen a young girl about fourteen years old with brown hair and a light blue t-shirt?"

"Yeah. She ran out of the theatre about a minute ago."

"Where'd she go?"

"She went that way," the ticket taker said, pointing to his right.

Maria ran to the sidewalk and looked down the street.

"Mom!" Cassandra yelled from half a block away.

Maria ran toward Cassandra. When she was about five feet from her, there was an enormous explosion. Grabbing Cassandra and pulling her to the ground, she covered her daughter with her own body. Debris was flying everywhere.

Thick black smoke billowed from the theatre. Screams could be heard from inside. Flames shot up from the top of the movie house.

A police officer ran over to Maria. "Hey, lady, is that your car?" he asked.

Maria nodded.

"Get it out of here. You're blocking the entrance."

Running to the car, Maria and Cassandra got in. Maria started the engine and drove the car forward about fifty feet.

The sound of sirens filled the air. Fire engines appeared, stopping in front of the theatre. Jumping off their trucks, the firemen started unrolling fire hoses and rushed in through the front entrance of the theatre. A fireman connected one of the hoses to a fire hydrant and turned it on using a huge wrench. Several firemen, carrying axes, ran to the side of the theatre and started breaking down the jammed exit doors. Black smoke billowed out from the open doors. By now, there was not much screaming. Several movie patrons lay unconscious on the floor next to the exit doors.

Ambulances began arriving on the scene. Paramedics quickly set up a triage area in front of the theatre. Firemen, policemen and paramedics carried victims to the street, where they were evaluated and treated. Covered with soot and looking dazed, a handful of people were able to walk out of theatre, assisted by emergency personnel.

Maria and Cassandra sat in the car.

"Mom, it happened just like I saw it," Cassandra said, starting to cry. "The same scene and everything."

"I know, honey."

"I couldn't get Tiffany and Cindy to leave," Cassandra said. "I tried, but they kept telling me to be quiet."

"I'm sure you tried, honey. It's not your fault."

More ambulances arrived on the scene as the fire grew in intensity.

"I have to see if Tiffany and Cindy are okay," Cassandra said, starting to get out of the car.

At that moment, a policeman appeared carrying yellow 'Police Line' tape. "You folks are going to have to leave," he said to Maria, through her partially opened window.

"This area is being secured."

"Come on, honey. Get back in the car."

As Maria drove away, the flashing lights of the fire engines, patrol cars and ambulances faded in the rear view mirror.

"What about Tiffany and Cindy?" Cassandra asked.

"We'll call as soon as we get home."

*　　*　　*

"Crestview Memorial Hospital," Maria told the information operator. Grabbing a pen, she jotted down the telephone number on the back of an envelope lying on the kitchen counter. "Thank you," Maria said, ending the call, then dialing the number of the hospital. "It's busy, honey," she said.

Cassandra pressed the remote, turning on the television. There on the screen was the scene in front of the Majestic Theatre. A female reporter was interviewing the Fire Commissioner.

"I'm speaking with Commissioner Ron Williams of the Crestview Fire Department," she said into her microphone. "Tell me, Commissioner, is there any indication as to what might have caused the explosion?" Turning to the commissioner, she tilted the microphone toward him.

"At this time, the investigation is in its initial stages," the Commissioner said. "We have not, as yet, determined the exact cause of the explosion. Based on the information that we have at this time, we believe that there was a rupture in the gas main that runs under the theatre. The gas was ignited, resulting in an explosion. As to the cause of ignition… I would only be speculating."

The reporter drew the microphone back to herself. "Thank you, Commissioner."

Commissioner Williams turned and re-joined the firemen at the scene.

The reporter continued, "This has been the worst disaster to hit Crestview in over fifty years. Not since the explosion at the Taylor Tire Factory in 1969, has a catastrophe of such magnitude occurred. This is Veronica Velasquez at the Majestic Theatre in Crestview, New Jersey. Back to you, Chuck."

"Thanks, Veronica. We'll be checking back with you as this story develops."

"Mom, call Tiffany's mother," Cassandra said, lowering the volume on the television.

Maria dialed the number and listened as the phone rang several times. "There's no answer, honey," Maria said, hanging up the receiver.

Turning back to the television, Cassandra raised the volume.

Chuck Brown, the news anchor, was speaking. "I have an update on the casualties resulting from the explosion at the Majestic Theatre. Being that it was a Saturday afternoon matinee, many of the victims were children. At this time, there are seven fatalities. About forty people have been seriously injured, some in critical condition. Many of the victims are being treated for smoke inhalation. Altogether, about one hundred and forty people have been transported to local area hospitals."

Getting emotional, Chuck shuffled the stack of papers on the desk in front of him, cleared his throat and said,

"Our hearts and prayers go out to the families and victims of today's tragedy. This is Chuck Brown, WMGM-TV, News 5, all the news, all the time, as it happens. We now return to our regular programming."

The telephone rang, startling both Maria and Cassandra. Maria reached for the phone. "Hello?"

"It's me," Nikos said.

"Nikos!"

Cassandra froze, holding her breath.

"How's Cassandra?"

"She's fine. She's right here."

"I just got to the hotel and turned on the news. Wasn't she at that theatre?"

"Yes," Maria answered. "But she wasn't feeling well and called me to pick her up."

"Let me talk to her."

"Daddy wants to talk to you, honey. Turn down the TV."

Lowering the volume on the television set, Cassandra walked over to Maria, who handed her the phone.

"Hi, Dad," Cassandra said, feigning cheeriness in her voice.

"Hi, sweetheart. How are you?"

"I'm fine. Here's Mom," Cassandra said, quickly handing the phone back to Maria.

"I told you she was all right."

"Is there anything else I should know?" Nikos asked.

"Like what?"

"Did she have another seizure?"

"No, she didn't have a seizure."

Cassandra looked at Maria, her face pale.

"Are you lying to me?" Nikos asked, pressing the issue.

"No," Maria said, looking at Cassandra. "I'm not lying."

"Do you want me to come home tonight?"

"No, it's okay. We'll be fine."

"I'll be home Monday night. I'm going to make an appointment with the new doctor."

Maria remained quiet.

"Bye," Nikos said.

"Bye." Maria hung up the phone.

"He wants me to go to that new doctor, doesn't he?" Cassandra said.

"Yes."

"I don't want to go, Mom."

"I know you don't."

~ Cassandra ~

Chapter Eight

THE EXORCISM

Lying in bed, Cassandra stared out her window at the overcast morning sky. She had been awakened by the sound of her mother talking on the phone. A few moments later, Maria appeared in the doorway, a despondent look on her face.

"Honey. I have some sad news."

"What is it?" Cassandra asked, sitting up in bed.

"That was Tiffany's aunt on the phone." Maria paused a moment. "Honey… Tiffany and Cindy didn't make it."

"What do you mean?" Cassandra asked, alarmed.

"They both died."

"Died?"

"Yes... from smoke inhalation."

Cassandra sat staring at Maria, tears welling up in her eyes.

"I'm sorry, honey," Maria said.

"I tried to get them to leave, but they wouldn't listen to me."

Maria and Cassandra were quiet for a moment.

"Mom?" Cassandra said, breaking the silence.

"Yes, honey?"

"I want to see Father George."

"I'll call him right now," Maria said.

*　*　*

Six marble sconces shed a soft light on the walls of the East Chapel of St. Sophia's Cathedral, giving the room a warm and inviting feeling. Four wooden pews with velvet cushions faced the small altar, above and behind which was a stained-glass window. On the walls, icons representing religions scenes were flanked by long crimson velvet drapes.

Father George, Peter, Maria and Cassandra stood near the small altar.

"Are you ready?" Father George asked, placing a small prayer book next to the large Bible resting on the altar table.

Cassandra nodded.

Walking over to where Cassandra was standing, Father George took her gently by the arm and led her to the altar table. "I want you to stand right here and place both of your hands on this Bible and face me."

As Cassandra placed both of her hands, palms down, on the Bible, a loud crack of thunder shook the chapel. A flash of lightning illuminated the stained glass window. The lights dimmed momentarily.

Father George opened his prayer book to a page which he had previously bookmarked. Holding the prayer book in his left hand, he reached across the altar table, placing his right hand on Cassandra's forehead. He began the prayer:

"In Thy name, O Lord, God of truth, I lay my hand upon Thy servant, who has been found worthy to seek refuge in Thy Holy Name…"

There was a crack of thunder. The lights in the chapel flickered.

"… and to be sheltered under the shadow of Thy wings. Take from her that ancient error and…"

There was another loud clap of thunder. The storm seemed to be directly above the chapel. The lights dimmed again. The storm appeared to become more violent with each passing moment.

Maria, feeling faint, sat down in one of the pews.

Father George continued, "… and fill her with Thy faith and hope and love that she may know Thou Alone art true God."

A deafening clap of thunder shook the walls of the chapel. The lights went out. A few lit candles on the altar remained the only source of light in the room.

Suddenly Cassandra's hands dropped to her sides. Her fists clenched. Her eyes opened wide, unblinking. Her whole body stiffened. As she started to speak, the voice that came forth sounded a little like Cassandra's, but was deeper, huskier.

"Oh… oh." Her mouth opened and closed sporadically. She gasped, then said something that sounded like "Ochi." Cassandra repeated the word. "Ochi."

Father George concentrated hard. Suddenly it hit him. He turned to Maria. "Does she know any Greek?"

"No. Not a word."

Cassandra continued to speak, in the same, strange sounding voice. "O Apóllon! O, o! Ochi, óchi, óchi, óchi! O gi!"

Terrified, Maria got up from her chair and started walking toward her daughter.

Father George gestured for her to stop. "Don't touch her!" he said firmly. "Let it come out."

Suddenly Cassandra cried out, "O, o! O tromos! O gi! O Apóllonas, o Apóllonas!"

Suddenly, the sound of glass breaking could be heard as the stained-glass window behind the altar shattered, allowing the ferocity of the storm to enter the chapel, pieces of glass flying everywhere, the rain pouring in through the broken window. A blast of wind, hitting Father George in the chest, lifted him off the ground, hurling him against the wall with such force that he was momentarily stunned.

Maria, seeing that Cassandra was about to faint, rushed to her side, catching her just as she was about to fall.

Peter, rushing over to Father George, who was on the floor, slumped against the wall, noticed some blood on the priest's forehead. Grabbing a handkerchief from his pocket, he held it against the cut.

"Do you want me to call a doctor, Father?" Peter asked.

At that moment, the lights in the chapel came back on.

"No, I'm alright," Father George, said, slowly getting to his feet. "Just see to Cassandra."

Peter walked over to Cassandra, who was lying on the floor, cradled in Maria's arms.

Cassandra opened her eyes, appearing dazed and confused. Seeing the broken stained-glass window and the rain pouring through it, Cassandra looked at Maria and asked, "What happened?"

"You fainted," Maria said.

Cassandra looked skeptical.

"Do you think you can stand up?" Peter asked Cassandra.

She started to get up, her legs wobbly.

"Here, let me help you," he said, gently supporting her, helping her to her feet. Maria also stood up.

Father George walked over to where Cassandra was standing.

"Are you okay?" he asked.

"I think so." Cassandra said. "What happened to *you*?" she asked, noticing the cut on his forehead.

"It's just a scratch. No big deal."

Cassandra looked unconvinced.

As they started to leave the chapel, Maria pulled Father George aside. "What is it, Father? Is it the devil?"

"No. It's not Satan," he said. "But whatever it is, it's very powerful."

* * *

Entering the kitchen from the garage, Maria and Cassandra saw Nikos leaning against the counter, his arms folded across his chest. He was seething with anger.

"Hi, Dad," Cassandra said, trying to sound casual.

"You'd better go upstairs to your room. Your mother and I have something we have to talk about."

Cassandra looked at Maria.

"Go ahead, honey. It'll be alright," Maria assured her.

Reluctantly, Cassandra walked out of the kitchen heading for the stairs.

"Carlo saw your car in the church parking lot."

Cassandra stopped halfway up the stairs, trying to hear what Nikos was saying.

"I tried to call you five times," Nikos continued.

Maria said nothing.

"I called the church. The woman who answered the phone said that you and Cassandra were in the chapel with the priest. She said that she had been given instructions not to interrupt."

Maria did not respond. Walking over to her, Nikos grabbed her by the arm.

"Ow! You're hurting me," Maria cried out.

Cassandra turned and ran back down the stairs to the kitchen.

"What the hell were you doing that couldn't be interrupted?" Nikos bellowed. "How many times have I told you that you're not to go to that church?"

"Let go of her!" Cassandra demanded, standing in the doorway.

"Go to your room!" Nikos commanded.

"No. I will not," Cassandra declared, standing her ground.

Maria broke free from Nikos' grasp.

"Why don't you want us to go to church?" Cassandra asked, defiantly.

With fury in his eyes, Nikos stared at Cassandra, then Maria. "I've had it with you two." Storming out of the kitchen, he headed upstairs.

*   *   *

"What are you doing?" Maria asked, standing in the doorway, watching Nikos throw articles of clothing into an open suitcase on the bed.

"I'm packing."

"I can see that. Where are you going?"

"I'm getting the hell out of here." Closing the suitcase, he picked it up and walked toward the door. Maria stepped aside as Nikos walked out of the bedroom and down the stairs. Moments later, she could hear the sound of the garage door opening, followed by the squeal of tires.

~ Cassandra ~

Chapter Nine

THE PSYCHIC

The morning sun was streaming in through Cassandra's bedroom window as she stood talking with Tony on her cell phone.

"A psychic?" Cassandra asked.

"Yes. She's supposed to be terrific," Tony answered. "She does a lot of work with the police. I made an appointment for three o'clock. I told her I'd call her back to confirm it."

"What could a psychic do?"

"She might be able to help. I think it's worth a try."

"Okay," Cassandra said.

"She said to bring something from each of your parents."

"What for?"

"I don't know," Tony said. "Can you be ready in half an hour?"

*   *   *

351 West 83rd Street was an old, five-story brownstone that had not yet been renovated. Tony and Cassandra climbed up the steps to the front door. Pressing the buzzer for apartment 2-B, Tony waited.

"Who is it?" a voice asked over the crackling sound of the intercom.

"It's Tony Petrarkos."

The front door lock started to buzz. Tony quickly pushed the door open before the buzzing could stop. He and Cassandra entered the old building. The aroma of cabbage cooking mixed with the musty smell of the carpeted hallway as they made their way up the stairs to the second floor.

"This way," Tony said, turning right at the top of the stairs. Cassandra followed.

Stopping in front of the door marked 2-B, Tony pressed the buzzer. Cassandra felt herself getting nervous. After a few moments, the door opened.

Katrina Vanderberg, in her late-forties, with graying blonde hair and gray-green eyes, stood in the doorway. She was dressed in a tan skirt and white blouse.

"Ms. Vanderberg?" Tony asked.

"Call me Katrina," she said, her voice warm, friendly. "You must be Tony."

"Yes… and this is Cassandra," Tony said.

Cassandra smiled, shyly.

"Please, come in," Katrina said, holding the door. Closing the door behind them, she turned the latch. "Can I get you some water or herb tea?"

"Water's fine, thank you," Tony said.

Katrina looked at Cassandra.

"For me, too. Thanks."

Katrina disappeared into the kitchen.

The apartment was filled with antiques, overstuffed furniture and books. Nearly all of the lamps in the apartment were switched on as the surrounding larger buildings blocked most of the sunlight.

Katrina returned with two small bottles of Evian water. "Would you like a glass?" she asked, handing the two bottles to Tony and Cassandra.

"No, this is perfect," Tony said.

"Me, too," Cassandra said.

"Let's go into my study," Katrina said, leading them into a softly lit, very comfortable-feeling room. The drapes had been drawn to block out whatever sunlight had managed to reach the window, in front of which, stood and old wooden desk facing two overstuffed chairs. A small sofa had been placed against one of the walls. The remaining walls were lined with shelves filled with books.

"Please, have a seat," Katrina said, motioning to the two chairs in front of her desk. Walking around her desk, she took a seat facing Tony and Cassandra.

Katrina turned to Tony and said, "Once we get started, I'm going to ask you to wait in the other room,"

"Oh, please. Can't he stay?" Cassandra asked, pleadingly.

"Is that what you want?"

"Yes, please."

Katrina looked at Cassandra, then Tony. "Very well. But you'll have to sit over there," she said to Tony, indicating the small sofa next to the wall. "You'll have to be very quiet. It should almost be as though you're not even in the room."

"I understand," Tony said.

Katrina turned her attention back to Cassandra. "Now, tell me, my dear. Why is it that you've come to see me?"

"I see things before they happen."

"Like what?"

"The other day, there was an explosion at the movie theater in Crestview."

"Yes. I heard about it on the news."

"Some friends of mine and I were in the theater. I knew it was going to happen. I tried to get them to leave, but they wouldn't listen to me."

"What happened then?"

"The manager of the theater threw me out for causing a disturbance. I was just trying to warn them."

"They didn't believe you?"

"No."

"And your friends?"

"They…" Cassandra eyes began to fill with tears. She could no longer hold back the emotions that had been welling up inside of her. "They died." she said, tears running down her cheeks.

"Go ahead. Let it out." Pulling a couple of tissues from a box on her desk, Katrina leaned forward, handing them to Cassandra. She waited while Cassandra dried her tears. After a few moments, Katrina asked, "Are you all right?"

"I guess so," Cassandra said, taking a sip of water from the Evian bottle.

"Tell me, my dear," Katrina continued, "when did all of this first start happening?"

"After the snake."

"The snake?" Katrina asked, concerned.

"Yes. I was four. We were just moving into our house on Oak Street. I was playing on the front lawn. That's when the snake came. Tony was there, too."

Glancing at Tony, Katrina asked, "You saw the snake?"

"Yes." Tony said, nodding.

"The next day, we went to the beach," Cassandra said.

"What happened at the beach?" Katrina asked, turning her attention back to Cassandra.

"I saw a boy drowning. I tried to scream, but no one could hear me."

Katrina took a sip of herb tea from a china mug. "What happened then?"

"We all left the beach. Tony and his mom, too. A few years later, my mother told me that a boy had drowned a few hours after I had seen it."

Katrina remained silent for a moment, thinking. "Did it ever happen again?"

"Nothing happened for the past ten years. Then it started up again last week. Three times."

"And the most recent event was the explosion at the

movie theater?"

"Yes."

"Have you talked to anyone about this?"

"I saw a neurologist, but he couldn't find anything wrong with me."

"Of course he couldn't. There's nothing wrong with you. On the contrary, you have a gift," Katrina said. "Precognition is a gift."

"But Dr. Zaren said that precognition is impossible."

Leaning forward on her elbows, Katrina said, "One thing that you have to understand about doctors is that their world is built around scientifically provable facts. It's nearly impossible to prove the existence of psychic phenomena."

"Then how come the police believe you?" Cassandra asked.

"They were skeptical at first. It wasn't until I was able to find evidence for them, again and again, that they finally began to believe me."

"Nobody except Tony and my Mom believe me."

"It's not your fault that people don't believe you. Precognition is a gift that has to be developed. Is there anyone else in your family who's precognitive?"

"No." Cassandra paused a moment, thinking. "What about you, Katrina? When did you know that you had psychic abilities?"

"When I was a little girl. It runs in my family. My mother had it. My grandmother had it, too. That's why I asked about your family." Sitting back in her chair, Katrina said, "We should get started. Did you bring something from each of your parents?"

Taking the ring and scarf out of her jeans pocket, Cassandra handed them to Katrina. Katrina briefly examined the ring. "Does your father know that you have this?" Katrina asked, putting the ring and scarf on her desk.

"No. He left last night."

"Left?"

"He and my Mom had a fight. He was angry with me, too. So he left."

"What was he angry about?"

"My mom had taken me to church."

"That's it?"

"Yes. He was furious."

Katrina took a sip of her tea. "Why had your mother taken you to church?"

"To see a priest."

"What for?"

"So he could say some prayers."

"What kind of prayers?"

"My mom said that they were prayers for exorcism."

Tony sat listening on the edge of the couch, riveted.

"What happened then?" Katrina asked.

"I don't really remember everything that happened. My mom told me that I started speaking in a foreign language. Right after that, the stained-glass window in the chapel broke. Then a huge gust of wind came in and threw Father George against the wall. He got a big cut on his forehead. I don't know if it was from the glass or from hitting his head against the wall. I don't remember much else. My mother said that I had fainted."

"Does anyone remember what it was that you said at the time?"

"Father George wrote it down on a piece of paper."

"Can you get a me copy of it?"

"Sure."

"What happened after you saw Father George?"

"My father got really angry that we had gone to a priest so he packed a suitcase and left."

"And you haven't heard from him since?"

"No."

"I see. I think we can start now," Katrina said, getting up from her chair. "Tony? Would you please move over to the sofa while I'm working with Cassandra?"

"Sure," Tony said. Getting up, he walked over to the small sofa by the wall and sat down.

"Also, Tony, would you please turn off the room lights? It's that switch over there by the door."

Tony leaned over and flipped the light switch. All the lights in the room went out, except for the small amber-shaded lamp on Katrina's desk, which shed a gentle, golden light on Cassandra and Katrina.

Walking around her desk, Katrina went to the chair that Tony had been sitting in. She turned it so that it faced Cassandra. "Cassandra. Would you please turn your chair so that you're facing me?"

"Sure." Getting up, Cassandra turned the chair, then sat back down.

Sensing that Cassandra was anxious, Katrina asked, "Are you nervous?"

"A little."

"There's no need be," she said, reassuringly. "Have you ever done any meditation?"

"No, not really."

"Well, this is sort of like meditation. You don't have to do anything. Just try to relax. I'll do the rest."

Seeing that Cassandra was still tense, she added, "Don't worry. It won't hurt. You won't feel a thing."

Cassandra seemed to relax a little.

Tony sat tensely on the edge of the sofa, beginning to wonder whether or not he had done the right thing by bringing Cassandra here.

"Now, I want you to lean back."

Cassandra leaned back in the chair.

"Close your eyes and try to relax," Katrina said.

Cassandra closed her eyes.

"I want you to breathe deeply and steadily. Try to clear your mind of all thoughts. Pretend that you're about to fall asleep. Now, keeping your eyes closed, place your right hand in mine."

Cassandra reached forward with her right hand. Katrina took it.

"Keep breathing. Are you feeling drowsy?"

"A little," Cassandra said.

Noticing that Cassandra was holding her breath, Katrina said, "Try not to hold your breath. Just breathe slowly and steadily."

A shadow passed over Katrina's face. "I'm getting some kind of interference."

Letting go of Katrina's hand, Cassandra leaned back in her chair and opened her eyes.

"Let's try again," Katrina said. "Give me your hand and close your eyes."

Reaching forward with her right hand, Cassandra closed her eyes. Katrina, once again, took Cassandra's hand, closed her eyes, and began to concentrate.

Tony watched from the sofa as Katrina and Cassandra sat in their chairs, facing one another.

Katrina, eyes closed, slowly began to nod her head, as if in acknowledgement of what it was that she was seeing. After a few minutes, Katrina released Cassandra's hand and sat back in her chair.

"You can open your eyes now."

Cassandra opened her eyes and looked at Katrina.

"How do you feel?"

"Okay, I guess."

"I saw your mother and father," Katrina said. "They were from a land very far away."

"Yes, they're from Greece."

"No," Katrina said, chuckling slightly. "I don't mean your present mother and father."

Cassandra looked at Katrina, not understanding. "What do you mean?"

"I'm talking about a long time ago. In fact, over three thousand years ago."

Cassandra's eyes opened wide.

"Your father's name was Priam. He was the king of Troy. And your mother, Hecuba, was the queen. I saw you playing with your brothers and sisters in the courtyard near the palace wall."

"But I don't have any brothers or sisters."

"You did then. You were a princess, my dear."

Cassandra stared at Katrina, still not understanding.

"Wait right here." Getting up from her chair, Katrina walked over to an old mahogany cabinet. Opening the cabinet door, she pulled out a small drawer and visually scanned its contents. Retrieving a small stone from the drawer, she returned to her seat.

"Here. Take this," she said, handing the stone to Cassandra. "Hold it in your hand. Now. Just like before, I want you to sit back and relax. This time, I want you close your eyes and concentrate on the stone."

Holding the stone in her hand, Cassandra sat back in the chair and closed her eyes.

"Just concentrate on the stone." Karina watched Cassandra's face intently. After a few moments, she noticed a tear running down Cassandra's cheek.

"Without opening your eyes, tell me what you feel. Where do you think the stone is from?"

"It's from the wall where I used to play when I was a child," Cassandra said, her voice filled with emotion. "I was very happy then."

Katrina looked pleased. "Okay. You can open your eyes now."

Cassandra slowly opened her eyes.

Taking the stone back from Cassandra, she placed it on her desk.

"You've done very well. How are you feeling?"

"A little tired."

"That's only natural." Reaching over to her desk, Katrina picked up the scarf. "Let's take a look at what you've brought." Closing her eyes, she held the scarf. A gentle smile came over Katrina's face. "Your mother loves you very much."

Cassandra nodded.

Putting the scarf back down on her desk, she picked up the ring, taking note of the strange markings on the stone. Katrina closed her eyes and leaned back in her chair. She seemed to be concentrating on something. It was night. Twelve hooded figures were making their way, down a narrow path that wound along a rocky cliff. They were carrying torches and were chanting in low voices as they made their way toward the beach. Katrina could see the faces of the young men in the light of the flickering torches.

Suddenly there was a loud pop. The light bulb in the lamp on Katrina's desk exploded, immersing the room in total darkness. Katrina screamed out in pain, dropping the ring to the floor. "Tony. Turn on the lights."

Tony leaned over and switched on the lights.

Katrina held out her hand.

"You're hurt," Cassandra exclaimed, alarmed, seeing a circular red mark on the palm of Katrina's hand.

"It's a burn," Katrina said. "Tony, could you please go to the kitchen and get me a piece of ice from the fridge?"

"Of course," Tony said, heading for the kitchen.

Cassandra, holding Katrina's hand, looked at the red burn mark on her palm. "It's looks pretty bad," Cassandra said.

Returning to the study, Tony handed the ice cube to Katrina. She pressed it against the burn on her palm.

Still holding the piece of ice, Katrina bent down and picked up the ring. She held Nikos' ring in her hand for a moment.

"Where did your father get this?" she asked Cassandra.

"I don't know."

A look of concern came over Katrina's face. Taking the scarf from the top of the desk, she handed both the scarf and ring back to Cassandra. "I'd like to see you again. Would that be okay with you?"

Cassandra nodded.

"I have Monday afternoon open. Can you make it?"

Cassandra looked questioningly at Tony. He nodded.

"Yes," Cassandra replied.

"Do you think that you could bring the ring with you?" Katrina asked, putting the ice cube on the saucer of the teacup resting on her desk.

"I think so."

"You're very special, my dear. I want to try to help you," Katrina said, giving Cassandra a warm hug. She then accompanied both Tony and Cassandra to the front door. "Take care," she said, holding the door open. "See you Monday." Tony and Cassandra stepped into the hallway. Katrina closed the door after them.

Tony and Cassandra started walking toward the stairway. Suddenly Tony stopped. "Wait here a second," he said to Cassandra. Turning, he walked back to Katrina's apartment.

He knocked on the door. "Katrina? It's Tony."

From inside, he heard, "Yes, Tony. I'm coming." The door opened. "Did you forget something?" Katrina asked.

"I need to ask you something," Tony said, stepping into the apartment.

"Sure. What is it?"

"That stone that came from the wall where Cassandra used to play when she was a little girl... ?"

"Yes?"

"Cassandra and I used to play by that wall when we were kids. Her house is two over from mine... on Oak Street. How did you get a stone from the wall on Oak Street?"

"Oak Street? Tony, that stone is from the wall that surrounded the palace in the ancient city of Troy... not Oak Street."

Tony felt a chill run up his spine. He stood, staring at Katrina.

Opening the door wider, Katrina saw Cassandra sitting on the top step waiting for Tony. Placing her hand on Tony's shoulder, Katrina said, "Go... she needs you."

Chapter Ten

PROFESSOR MENDELSON

Their footsteps echoed throughout the corridors of the old Columbia University building as Tony and Cassandra made their way up the marble stairs to Professor Mendelson's office. It being Sunday, the building was empty, save for a few professors and graduate students catching up on work before summer session was due to begin.

"Why is the professor here on a Sunday?" Cassandra asked.

"He told me this morning, when we spoke on the phone, that he's going to be leaving for upstate tomorrow. This is our only chance to see him. He's here because he has to gather up some materials for an essay that he's working on."

"What floor is he on?" Cassandra asked, trudging up the stairs.

"Just one more flight." Tony continued, "Anyway, I was asking Dad if he knew anything about Troy... he knows I'm reading Homer and all that. He told me that he really didn't know that much, but that he knew someone who did. And that's Professor Mendelson. He and my father have been friends for years. Dad told me to call him, so I did."

Tony and Cassandra continued to make their way up the stairs.

"By the way, do you have that piece of paper with the stuff that Father George wrote on it?"

"Yes. Why did you want me to bring it?"

"The professor may know how to interpret it."

"What did you tell him about it?" she asked, handing the piece of paper to Tony.

"I told him that during a prayer session with a priest, that you had spoken in a foreign language." Looking at Cassandra, Tony asked, "Did I say the wrong thing?"

"No, that's exactly what happened."

Tony took the folded piece of paper and put it in the back pocket of his chinos. As they reached the landing on the third floor, he looked to the left, then to the right, checking out the room numbers.

"There it is," Tony said. He and Cassandra approached an open door. Inside, sitting at an old battered desk was the man they'd come to see. Edward Mendelson, in his mid-fifties, with slightly graying hair, reading glasses perched on his nose, was sorting through one of the many piles of papers on the desk.

"Professor Mendelson?" Tony asked, rapping on the doorframe with his knuckle.

"You must be Tony," Professor Mendelson said, looking up at him over the top of his glasses. "I'm so glad that you could make it." Getting up from his desk, he walked over to Tony and Cassandra, his right hand extended.

Tony shook his hand, then said, "This is Cassandra."

"Pleased to meet you, Cassandra," Edward said, extending his hand to her.

"Same here," Cassandra said shyly, shaking his hand.

"Come on. Let's sit down." Edward arranged two wooden chairs in front of his desk for Tony and Cassandra. "How are your parents? I haven't seen them for quite some time."

Tony smiled. "They're fine. I'll tell them that you asked about them.

Edward's face got serious. "Now, Tony, you were telling me about something on the phone... ."

"Yes," Tony said. Reaching into his pocket, he retrieved the folded piece of paper and handed it to Edward.

Edward unfolded the piece of paper, which read:

Ο Απόλλων! Ω, ω! Οχι, όχι, όχι, όχι! Ω γη!
Ω, ω! Ο τρόμος! Ω γη! Ο Απόλλωνας, ο Απόλλωνας!

Turning to Cassandra, Edward asked, "Do you speak Greek?"

"No."

"Not at all?"

"Not at all."

"Interesting," Edward mused. "I'd like to show this to a friend of mine. He's a professor who teaches ancient Greek. Would that be alright with you?"

"Sure."

Picking up the receiver of the phone on his desk, Edward dialed a number.

"Hey, Neil. It's Edward Mendelson. I wasn't sure whether or not you'd be in today." He paused and listened. "Yes, I know exactly what you mean. I don't think I'll ever catch up. Listen, Neil, I have a few lines written in Greek that I'd like for you to translate for me. Can I fax them over to you?" He listened for a moment. "Sure. Do you want me to wait until you get back, or should I do it now?" Edward paused. "Great." Hanging up the phone, he got up and went over to the fax machine, which rested on a file cabinet in the corner.

"He said that he has to step out of his office for a few minutes," Edward told Tony and Cassandra, "but he'll fax us as soon as he gets back."

Carefully placing the piece of paper in a see-through plastic carrier, Edward positioned it in the fax machine. Dialing Neil's fax number, he pressed 'Fax Start'.

In the distance, a low rumble of thunder could be heard. The sky began to darken.

"And the forecast was for sunny weather," Edward commented, chuckling.

Upon completing the fax transmission, he returned to his desk and sat down, handing the piece of paper back to Tony.

"Cassandra?" Edward asked, turning to her.

"Yes, sir?"

"Tony said that your parents are from Greece."

"That's right."

"And they never spoke any Greek around the house?"

"Maybe when I was a baby. But I don't remember anything."

"Do you have any other relatives that speak Greek?"

"Yes, but we hardly ever see them, and when we do, they speak English."

Cassandra waited a moment and then asked, "Professor Mendelson?"

"Yes, Cassandra?"

"Who was Priam?"

"He was the king of Troy," Edward answered, surprised by the question. "Do you know anything about Troy?"

"Not really."

"It's not a functioning city anymore," Edward said, "but the ruins are still there."

Edward got up from his chair and walked over to a large, framed, parchment map hanging on the wall.

"Come look," Edward said. Getting up from their chairs, Tony and Cassandra walked over to where Edward was standing.

"Here." Edward pointed to a place on the map. "This is Troy. It's actually located in what today is Turkey."

Cassandra and Tony looked at the map, fascinated."

"Over here, across the Aegean Sea, is Greece. You can

see how it was possible to get from Greece to Troy by ship. Though, in those days, it took a very long time."

"You said that your parents were from Greece," Edward said, turning to Cassandra. "Do you know where exactly?"

"Telenos."

"That's right over here." Edward said, pointing to an island near the Greek mainland."

"I never saw it on a map before," Cassandra said, impressed.

Walking back to his chair, Edward asked, "Would you like some Perrier?"

"No, I'm okay," Tony said.

"Me, too," Cassandra said.

Sitting down at his desk, Edward took a sip from the open bottle of water.

Tony and Cassandra returned to their seats.

"Now, where were we?" Edward paused, thinking for a moment. "Yes... Priam. Well, King Priam and his wife, Hecuba, ruled Troy about three thousand years ago. They had many children, including a daughter who was your namesake... Cassandra."

Cassandra eyes opened wide.

"Legend has it that she was their most beautiful daughter," Edward said, "and that she had many suitors... including the god, Apollo."

"Apollo?" Cassandra asked.

"Yes. Apollo was so taken by Cassandra's beauty that he promised to give her the gift of prophecy if she would, in return, give him her love." Edward paused a moment.

He was clearly enjoying telling the story. He continued. "Cassandra agreed. So Apollo sent a snake that whispered in her ear, enabling her to see the future."

Tony and Cassandra looked at each other.

"But after Cassandra had received the gift of prophecy, she changed her mind."

"Uh oh," Cassandra said.

"Yes. She didn't keep her side of the bargain. This made Apollo very angry. Since he couldn't take back the gift he had given her, he cursed her so that no one would ever believe her."

"That's just like me," Cassandra murmured, half to herself.

Edward looked at Cassandra, not knowing what she meant.

"Have you ever heard of the Trojan Horse?" Edward asked.

"A little… in school," she said.

Taking off his reading glasses, Edward leaned forward, resting his elbows on the desk.

"The Greeks were unable to defeat the Trojans in battle. The city of Troy was on higher ground and very well fortified. The only way that the Greeks could prevail over the Trojans was to trick them. So they built a giant wooden horse and hid some soldiers inside. They left the horse in front of the gate to the city. The Trojans, thinking it was a gift, brought the horse inside the gate."

Cassandra and Tony sat listening, attentively.

"That night, while everyone in the city was asleep, the Greek soldiers climbed out of the wooden horse and opened the gate. The Greek army, which had been wait-ing in hiding on the beach, came in through the open gate. They killed nearly all of the Trojans and burned the city to the ground."

Cassandra sat motionless, listening.

Edward continued, "Cassandra had tried to warn the Trojans about the wooden horse… but no one believed her."

Cassandra gasped, her face pale. *That **is** just like me*, she thought to herself. "What happened to the King and Queen?" she asked.

"They were killed."

"And Cassandra?"

"She was taken as slave by Agamemnon. He was the king of Greece and general of the Greek army. When Agamemnon and his army returned to Greece, Cassan-dra warned that his wife, Clytemnestra, was going to kill him... and herself, Cassandra, as well."

"And?" Cassandra asked.

"It happened. Just like she said it would."

Cassandra looked ashen.

Just then, the fax machine started printing. "Ah! Here it is," Edward said, getting up from his chair and walking over to the machine.

As he started to retrieve the printout, a loud crack of thunder shook the room. Raindrops started coming in through the open window. "Just my luck," Edward said, walking over to the window and closing it. "I didn't bring an umbrella."

He has no idea, Cassandra thought.

Putting on his reading glasses, Edward read the fax, transfixed. Walking back over to his desk, he sat down.

"This is incredible," he mumbled under his breath. Reaching for one of the books piled on his desk, he opened it and flipped through the pages, as if looking for something.

Tony and Cassandra watched him intently.

Edward stopped turning the pages. "Here." He began to read aloud:

"O Apollo! Oh, oh! No, no, no, no! O earth! Oh, oh! O horror! O earth! O Apollo, Apollo!"

A loud crack of thunder rattled the room. Rain pelted the window with a fury.

Oh no! It's happening again, Cassandra thought, tensing up.

Edward turned the book around so that Tony could see the page right side up, and handed it to him. "Look at the page on the left," he said, excitement in his voice.

Tony studied the page:

Ο Απόλλων! Ω, ω! Οχι, όχι, όχι, όχι! Ω γη!
Ω, ω! Ο τρόμος! Ω γη! Ο Απόλλωνας, ο Απόλλωνας!

"I can't read it. It's in Greek."

"Now, compare it to the writing on the piece of paper that you brought to me."

Tony retrieved the note from his pocket. Unfolding the piece of paper, he looked at what Father George had written on it:

Ο Απόλλων! Ω, ω! Οχι, όχι, όχι, όχι! Ω γη!
Ω, ω! Ο τρόμος! Ω γη! Ο Απόλλωνας, ο Απόλλωνας!

Tony held the piece of paper next to the book and studied it for a moment. He looked at the book... then at the piece of paper... then at the book again. "They're the same."

"Yes... exactly!" Edward said.

Suddenly, there was the sound of breaking glass. The window shattered as though it has been struck by a rock.

Cassandra flashed back to the chapel in St. Sophia's Cathedral. She saw the shattered pieces of the stained glass window flying through the air. Father George was hurled against the wall.

"Cassandra?" Tony's voice brought her back to the present.

"Huh?" she replied, slightly disoriented.

"Are you okay?" Tony asked.

At that moment, a strong gust of wind rushed through the broken window, swirling around Professor Mendelson's desk, scattering papers everywhere. Edward tried in vain to keep whatever papers were left on his desk from being blown away.

Rushing to help Edward pick up his papers, Cassandra said, "I'm so sorry."

"Why? It's not your fault," he said.

Oh, yes it is, she thought to herself.

Cassandra and Tony collected the remaining papers, stacking them neatly on Edward's desk.

"Thank you," he said, opening his brief case and putting some papers into it.

"We've taken too much of your time," Tony said, apologetically.

"No. No. It's been my pleasure."

"Can we give you a lift home?" Tony asked.

Edward walked over to the window and looked out. The wind had died down. A light rain was falling. "No thanks. I'll be all right." Stepping away from the window, he heard the sound of broken glass crunch under his shoes. Looking down at the pieces of glass on the floor, he said, "I'd better give maintenance a call and have them take care of this before someone gets hurt."

"Thanks again, Professor," Tony said, as he and Cassandra headed for the door.

"Take care," Edward said. "Have a good summer and be sure to say hi to your folks for me."

"I will," Tony said.

Suddenly, Cassandra stopped and turned in the doorway. "Professor Mendelson?"

"Yes?"

"Did people really believe that Apollo existed back then?"

"Yes, they did."

"Do people still believe in Apollo?"

"No. That ended over two-thousand years ago."

Cassandra thought for a moment.

"Yes, Cassandra?" Edward asked, sensing that she had something else to ask him.

"Just because people don't believe in Apollo anymore... does that mean that he doesn't exist?"

Closing his briefcase, Edward looked at Cassandra. "You know, I've never been asked that question before." He paused a moment. "I'll have to think about it."

~ Cassandra ~

Chapter Eleven

KATRINA AND TONY

Stepping out of the shower, Cassandra heard the door-bell chime. Slipping into her bathrobe, she headed for the stairs.

"I'll get it," Maria called up to her.

Cassandra could hear her mother talking to someone at the front door, but was unable to make out what was being said. It sounded as though Maria was questioning a delivery of some sort. Quickly putting on a pair of jeans and a clean t-shirt, Cassandra headed downstairs. Her mother was standing at the opened front door, looking pale.

"What's going on?" Cassandra asked, seeing a female uniformed officer walking away toward an official-looking car parked at the curb.

"Your father just served me with divorce papers," Maria said, handing the opened, oversized envelope to Cassandra.

"Divorce papers?"

"He claims that we have irreconcilable differences. He's also suggesting that I'm a bad influence on you."

"That's crazy."

"I know."

"Come on, Mom. Let's go into the kitchen." Taking her mother by the arm, Cassandra led her to the kitchen. Maria sat down at the table, watching numbly as Cassandra poured her a cup of coffee. "I can't believe it," Cassandra said, placing the cup in front of Maria.

"He's going for custody, too," Maria said, taking a sip of the coffee.

"Custody?! He can't do that! I'm going to be fifteen in less than two weeks."

"You're still a minor until you're eighteen."

"But there's no reason for him to claim custody," Cassandra insisted.

"The papers say, 'conflicting religious beliefs'."

"What? He's never even been to church."

"It doesn't matter, honey. When it comes to custody, religion is an important issue."

"But how can he do that?"

"He's using Stavros' law firm. They're very powerful. They almost always win in court."

Maria began to cry. "Honey, I don't want to lose you."

Walking over to her mother, Cassandra put her arms around her, hugging her tightly. "You're not going to lose me, Mom. I'm going to fight this. I want to stay with you... not Dad."

Suddenly, Cassandra heard Tony's ring tone on her cell phone. She answered the call. "Hi, Tony. Hold on a minute." Turning to Maria, she said, "I'll be right back." Maria nodded. Walking into the den, Cassandra spoke into the phone. "Okay. I can talk now."

"What's the matter?" Tony asked.

"I can't make it to Katrina's today. Dad just served Mom with divorce papers. I've got to stay here with her. She's really shaken up."

"Don't worry about Katrina. I'll call and tell her that you can't make it."

"But what about the note from Father George?"

"I still have it in my pocket. I can drop it off."

"And she wanted to see the ring again," Cassandra said, opening the desk drawer in which she had found the ring. "Tony, the ring's not here!"

"Don't worry. I'll figure something out."

"Thanks. Let me know what happens."

"I will."

*　　*　　*

"Come in, Tony. I'm sorry that Cassandra was unable to come," Katrina said, closing the door behind him. "Did you bring the note?" she asked, as she and Tony walked into her study.

"Yes." Reaching into his pocket, Tony retrieved the

note and handed it to Katrina. "We found out what it means. Yesterday we saw a professor at Columbia University. He said that it's a quote from the Greek play, Agamemnon, where Cassandra called out to Apollo... just before she was killed."

Katrina studied the note for a moment, then put it on her desk. "Did you bring the ring?"

"Cassandra couldn't find it," Tony said. "So I brought something else instead. I hope it'll work." Reaching into his pocket, Tony withdrew three small plastic envelopes, each containing an ancient Greek coin. "These coins have been untouched by anyone since Cassandra's father gave them to my dad about five years ago."

Taking the envelopes from Tony, Katrina put them on her desk. "I'll take a look at these later."

"I'd better get going," Tony said. "I don't want to take your time."

"No problem at all. In fact, I'm very curious about something. Would you mind if I did a reading on you?"

"Of course not."

Katrina moved the two overstuffed chairs in front of her desk so that they faced each other.

"Please. Have a seat," Katrina said, gesturing to one of the chairs. Walking over to the light switch, she dimmed the lights, then returned to her chair. Tony and Katrina sat down, facing one another.

"Try to relax. Close your eyes. Breathe slowly and steadily."

Closing his eyes, Tony sat back in his chair.

"Now, give me your right hand... just like Cassandra

did."

Tony extended his hand to Katrina. Taking his hand in hers, she leaned back and closed her eyes. Katrina began nodding her head in acknowledgement of what she was seeing.

After a few moments, she let go of Tony's hand. "You can open you eyes now," she said.

"Am I royalty, too?" Tony asked, half-jokingly.

Katrina smiled. "No, I'm afraid not. But you were close to it. Cassandra had a brother, Helenus. You were his best friend. And you were in love with Cassandra... even then."

Tony looked at Katrina, blushing.

"Don't try to hide it, my dear," she said. "It's written all over you."

"Do you think Cassandra knows?"

"I'm not sure. You two have been friends for such a long time." Katrina paused. "No matter what, I bet she feels the same way about you... but is just too shy to show it." Katrina took a sip from the glass of water on her desk. "Anyway, you were in love with her then," she said, putting the glass back on the desk. "But you were sixteen and had to join the army to fight in the war against Greece. You were away for two years. When you returned, Troy had already been destroyed and Cassandra had been taken as a slave to Greece."

"I know... by Agamemnon."

Katrina nodded, then said, "And then she was killed."

"I was too late."

"Yes. You were."

They both sat quietly for a moment, looking at each other.

A look of concern passed over Katrina's face. "Tony, when you first told me about Cassandra, you mentioned that her family was from Telenos."

"That's right."

"Do you know anything about Telenos?"

"No, not a thing."

"I did some research since I last saw the both of you. Telenos has a strange reputation. It was once known as a place where they performed human sacrifices to pagan gods, in particular, child sacrifices."

"That's horrible," Tony remarked.

"Let's have a look at some of these coins," Katrina said, reaching over to her desk, picking up one of the plastic envelopes. "You're sure that no one has touched these coins since Cassandra's father gave them to your father?"

"I'm sure."

Slipping the coin out of its envelope, she placed it in the palm of her right hand, where the burn from Nikos' ring was still visible. Closing her fingers around the coin, she leaned back in her chair and closed her eyes.

Tony watched as Katrina nodded her head, wishing that he could see what she was seeing. The calm expression on her face was soon replaced by one of concern. After a few moments, she opened her eyes. "I still can't get past that point."

"What do you mean?"

"I'll tell you in a minute. At least it's working with the coin. It took me back to the same scene that I saw the other day with the ring."

Tony remained quiet.

"It was some kind of ceremony... a ritual of some sort. There were young men wearing black, hooded robes and carrying torches. They were chanting something. I couldn't make out what they were saying." She took another sip of water from the glass on her desk. "I heard the cries of a young boy. And then I lost it again. It felt like something was blocking me... trying to prevent me from seeing."

Tony sat, fascinated.

"Tony, I have a feeling that something bad happened in Telenos... and it's affecting Cassandra now." Katrina put the coin back in its envelope and took another one from its package. Again, holding the coin in the palm of her right hand, Katrina leaned back in her chair and closed her eyes.

Tony watched her. Suddenly Katrina opened her eyes and sat upright in her chair, agitated, tense.

"Tony, you've got to go to Greece... right away."

"What?"

"The answer is there... in Greece... but it won't be for much longer. I can't explain why I have this feeling of urgency, but I do. If you don't get the answer now, it may be lost forever."

* * *

Cassandra walked into the kitchen and saw her mother hanging up the phone.

"That was your father," Maria said, a numbness in her voice.

"What did he want?" Cassandra asked.

"He said he's coming by tomorrow to pick you up. He wants you to stay with his cousin Ted in Astoria until we get all this finalized."

"What's wrong with me staying here?"

"He thinks I'm a bad influence on you."

"That's crazy. I'm not going."

"You have to, honey."

"I'm not going." Cassandra said, a steely resolve in her voice.

Hearing Tony's ring tone on her cell phone, Cassandra quickly put the phone to her ear. "Tony. Where are you?"

"I'm on the Jersey Turnpike."

"What's happening?" Cassandra asked, walking out of the kitchen and into the hallway.

"I'm going to Greece."

"What?"

"Katrina told me that the answer is in Greece."

"The answer to what?"

"To what's happening. She said that I've got to go now. That there's not much time left."

"For what?"

"I don't know. She didn't say. She just said that it's important that I go now."

Cassandra was silent for a moment, then suddenly said, "I'm going with you."

"What?"

"There's going to be a custody hearing in three weeks." Cassandra lowered her voice so that Maria couldn't hear her. "I'm going with you."

"But you don't even have a passport."

"Oh, yes, I do. I've had one for over a year now. Last year when Uncle Mikéli got sick, Mom and I thought we'd have to go to Greece. He got better, but I ended up getting a passport anyway."

"How do you know your mother will let you go?"

"She won't. I won't tell her until we're at the airport."

"Are you sure you want to do this?"

"I'm positive."

"Okay. Can you be ready in an hour?"

~ Cassandra ~

Chapter Twelve

GREECE

Tony and Cassandra, seated next to each other on the American Airlines passenger jet, slept peacefully as the airliner made its way toward Greece. Cassandra's head was resting on Tony's shoulder, his arm around her.

"Ladies and gentlemen, we've begun our approach to Athens International Airport," the flight attendant's voice announced over the speaker. "Please fasten your seatbelts. Bring your seats and tray tables to their fully upright positions."

Tony nudged Cassandra gently. "Wake up," he whispered, removing his arm from around her shoulder.

"We're getting ready to land."

Cassandra opened her eyes, disoriented for a moment. Then she remembered that she and Tony were on a passenger jet to Greece.

"How long have I been asleep?" she asked.

"A couple of hours," he said, looking at the clock on his cell phone.

"Did you sleep, too?"

"A little." Tony felt his cell phone vibrate, indicating a text message. Looking at the display, he said, "It's my uncle. A driver is going to meet us at the gate. After we've cleared customs, he'll take us to Uncle Dan's office."

* * *

Cassandra and Tony sat looking at the display of a large laptop computer, which rested on a sleek, glass-topped desk in a spacious modern office. Daniel Petrarkos, 42 years old, Tony's uncle on his father's side, was one of the senior editors of The Athens News, the oldest English language newspaper in Greece. He walked over to where they were sitting.

"How's it going?" Dan asked, looking over Tony's shoulder as Tony stared at the display of the laptop.

"I think I'm going to need your help," Tony said. "All the news regarding Telenos is in Greek."

"Here. Let me take a look," Dan said.

Relinquishing his chair to Dan, Tony got up.

"What was the date of the wedding?" Dan asked, sitting down.

"August 26th," Cassandra said.

"And the names?" he asked.

"Maria Andreos and Nikos Theopoulos."

Making a few keystrokes, Dan went back sixteen years in the database. Hundreds of words, written in Greek, filled the display of the laptop.

"Telenos News," Dan read aloud. "Saturday, August 26th." Glancing at the headline, he said, "This is odd," then read aloud, "BOY MISSING FROM ORPHAN-AGE." He scrolled down the page. "Here. Wedding announcements: Maria Andreos and Nikos Theopoulos, both residents of Tibius, are to be married today at the Church of St. Ignatius."

"That's it!" Cassandra said, excitement in her voice.

"What's that headline story about the missing boy?" Tony asked. "Can you go back to it?"

"Sure," Dan said, scrolling back up to the article and reading aloud, "Boy missing from the Sisters of Mercy Orphanage." He continued. "Authorities have begun an investigation into the disappearance of a nine-year-old boy who was reported missing from the orphanage on the evening of Friday, August 25th."

"Can you get me a translation of that article?" Tony asked.

"Sure," Dan said, printing out the article. "I'll have my secretary do it for you." Leaning over to his intercom, he pushed a button and said, "Tina, would you please come into my office?"

Moments later an attractive brunette in her early thirties, wearing a navy skirt and white blouse, entered Dan's office.

"Yes, Mr. Petrarkos?" Tina asked.

"Would you please translate this article into English and print it out for my nephew?" Dan said, handing the article to Tina.

"Of course," Tina said, taking the printout from Dan. As she left the office, she smiled at Tony and Cassandra.

"Why do you want that article?" Cassandra asked.

"I'll tell you later," Tony said.

Moments later, Tina returned with the article printed out in English. She handed it to Dan.

"Thank you, Tina."

Tina smiled, then said to Dan, indicating Cassandra, "Eínai polý ómorfo."

"Yes," Dan nodded in agreement, as Tina left the office.

"What did she say?" Tony asked.

"She said that Cassandra is very beautiful."

Cassandra looked down, blushing.

"Uncle Dan, we have to call a taxi," Tony said. "We've got to get to Telenos."

"I thought you were going to stay over," Dan said, handing Tony the printout.

"I thought we were, too, but there's no time," Tony said, folding the news article and putting it in his back pocket.

"What's the hurry?" Dan asked.

"I'll tell you later." Tony began texting on his phone.

"Who are you texting?" Cassandra asked.

"Your uncle. I'm letting him know that we're coming this evening instead of tomorrow."

"I'll call a cab," Dan said. "The last plane to Telenos

leaves in about an hour."

*   *   *

"When was the last time you saw your uncle?" Tony asked, rolling down the window of the small taxicab.

"When I was four. Uncle Mikéli stayed with us for a few days in our apartment in Astoria. It was just before we moved to Oak Street."

"Was your father there?"

"No. He was out-of-town. I remember sleeping in my mother's room. Uncle Mikéli stayed in mine."

"Is your mother still close with him?"

"Not like she used to be. They used to talk a lot on the phone, but my father didn't like it. Now they just email once in while."

Tony and Cassandra looked out the windows of the taxicab as it made its way along the dusty, winding road that led up the hill to the Monastery of St. Ignatius, a modest group of whitewashed adobe buildings.

The taxi driver pulled up in front of the monastery. After paying the driver, Tony and Cassandra got out of the cab, each holding their small carry-on bag. The driver waved and pulled away.

Noticing that they were on a cliff, Tony walked toward the edge. "What a view!" he exclaimed, as the sun began setting over the Aegean Sea. "Come look!"

Cassandra walked over to where Tony was standing. "It's gorgeous," she said. Looking over the edge of the cliff, seeing the waves crashing against the rocks, hundreds of feet below, a sudden sense of vertigo overcame her. Grabbing Tony's arm, she said, "It makes me dizzy."

They both stepped back from the edge.

"Cassandra!"

Cassandra turned to see her uncle, Mikéli Andreos, thirty-six years old, wearing a priest's collar, a short-sleeved black shirt and black slacks, walking out to greet them.

Putting down her bag, Cassandra ran to Mikéli and gave him a big hug. "Uncle Mikéli!"

"I can't believe how much you've grown." Mikéli said, standing back and looking at her. "You look just like your mother when she was your age. I can't believe you're really here."

Cassandra smiled. Mikéli turned to Tony, extending his right hand. "You must be Tony," he said, shaking Tony's hand.

"Pleased to meet you, Father."

"Please, call me Mikéli."

The sound of church bells ringing announced evening vespers. Picking up Cassandra's bag, Mikéli said, "You must be hungry. Let me show you where you'll be staying. Vespers are about to begin. I'll join you in a little while. We can have a bite to eat then."

Cassandra and Tony followed Mikéli into the monastery.

* * *

A rustic table that served as a desk, a few wooden chairs and some bookcases filled with old books, were the only items of furniture in Mikéli's spartanly furnished office. A narrow window looked out onto the Aegean Sea.

Mikéli, Cassandra and Tony sat at the wooden table.

There was a loaf of bread, some cheese and fruit on a tray. The soothing sound of a hymn being sung by some of the priests in the church echoed throughout the building.

"I spoke with your mother," Mikéli said to Cassandra. "She was relieved to hear that you've arrived safely. She also said that your father is furious."

"I can believe it," Cassandra said.

"Tell me, Cassandra. Why have you come to Telenos? Certainly not to see your old uncle."

"You're not old," Cassandra said, smiling.

Mikéli chuckled for a moment, then his demeanor turned serious. "Your mother told me about the divorce papers. She's very upset."

"Did she tell you why my Father wants a divorce?"

"No. Why?"

"He doesn't want her taking me to church."

Mikéli was silent, a questioning look in his eyes.

"He was going to take me away from Mom," Cassandra said. "It would've been today. He was going to make me stay with his cousin in Astoria."

"I know," Mikéli said. "Your mother told me."

"I had to get away. That's why I wanted to come to Greece with Tony."

"You didn't stay in Athens very long," Mikéli said, turning to Tony.

"I know," Tony said. "I knew we had to get to Telenos as soon as possible."

"Why Telenos?"

"I need to find out some things," Tony said.

"Like what?" Mikéli asked.

"I'm not really sure. I just know that I have to be here," Tony said, touching the folded newspaper article in his back pocket.

Chapter Thirteen

TIBIUS

The afternoon sun baked down on the parched, rocky terrain of the island as the older model, white SUV turned off the main road onto a dirt road that led to the old fishing village of Tibius. The SUV came to a halt in front of a small grocery store. Mikéli, Tony and Cassandra stepped out of the vehicle.

"That's where your Mom and I grew up," Mikéli said, pointing to a small, one-story house, halfway down the small street.

"Can I go inside?" Cassandra asked.

"I don't know the people who live there now," Mikéli

said. "I don't really feel comfortable knocking on their door."

Alexio, the owner of the store, in his late forties, stepped out into the street. "Father Mikéli!"

"Alexio!" Mikéli called back.

Alexio walked over to the car and shook Mikéli's hand.

"This is my niece, Cassandra, and her friend, Tony. They're from America. I have to go into town for about an hour. Can I leave them in your care?"

"Of course, Father."

Alexio turned to Tony and Cassandra. "How about something cold to drink?"

"Sounds great," Tony said, beginning to feel the effect of the hot afternoon sun.

"Thanks, Alexio," Father Mikéli said. Getting back into his SUV, he waved and drove away.

Cassandra and Tony followed Alexio into his store. A seven-year-old boy with dark brown hair was standing in front of the candy display. He looked at Tony and Cassandra with curiosity.

"Peppi. These people are from America," Alexio said. "This is Father Mikéli's niece, Cassandra Andreos."

"My last name is Theopoulos," Cassandra said, correcting him. "Nikos is my father."

A look of concern came over Alexio's face. Peppi smiled shyly at Cassandra and Tony, then ran out of the store.

"That's Peppi, the great-grandson of Petros, the old fisherman. He's very shy." Reaching into the cooler, Alexio retrieved two bottles of Coca Cola, opened them and handed them to Tony and Cassandra. Tony instinctively reached for his wallet.

"No. No. You are my guests."

"Thanks," Tony said, taking a few gulps from the bottle and putting it back down on the counter. Cassandra, not thirsty, took a few sips from her Coke and placed it next to Tony's.

"Do you think it would be alright if we just walked around the village for a while?" Tony asked. "Cassandra wants to see where her parents grew up."

"Of course," Alexio said, walking to the door and stepping outside. Tony and Cassandra followed.

"That was your mother's house," Alexio said, pointing down the street.

"I know," Cassandra said. "Uncle Mikéli told me."

"And two houses down from that on the other side of the street is where your father lived."

*　　*　　*

Tony and Cassandra stood looking at the modest, but neatly kept, small white house where Maria spent her early years.

"I'd love to see inside," Cassandra said.

"We probably shouldn't disturb them. Your uncle said he doesn't know the people who live here now."

Tony and Cassandra walked down the street toward the house where Nikos used to live. It was smaller than Maria's house and looked run-down with weeds growing in the front yard. Cassandra and Tony stood in the street, looking at the house.

"I can't believe he's going to divorce her," Cassandra

said.

At that moment, Tony and Cassandra saw Peppi running up the street toward them. Out of breath, Peppi handed Tony a piece of paper. Taking the note, Tony read the words aloud, "Come with me."

"He wants us to go with him," Tony said to Cassandra.

Tony bent down to speak with Peppi. "Where do you want us to go?"

"Pappoú. Pappoú," Peppi said, excitedly.

Tony and Cassandra looked at Peppi, not understanding.

"Pappa. Pappa," Peppi said.

"That must be the old fisherman that Alexio mentioned," Tony said, straightening up.

"Why does he want to speak with us?" Cassandra asked.

Tony shrugged. "I don't know."

"Do you think we should we go?"

"Probably," Tony said. He looked at the boy. "Okay, Peppi. Let's go."

Peppi started running down the street. Cassandra and Tony followed. "Peppi, slow down," Tony called to the little boy.

* * *

At the end of the path stood a small, whitewashed, one-bedroom house. The front door was opened wide, in order to take advantage of the breeze coming in off the sea. Following Peppi, Tony and Cassandra crossed the threshold into Petros' house. They stood still for a moment, waiting for their vision to adjust to the dark interior.

"I am Petros," a voice said. "I prayed that you would come. God has answered my prayers."

Petros, in his late eighties, with a weather-beaten face, stepped forward, extending his right hand to Tony.

"I'm Tony," Tony said, shaking Petros' calloused right hand.

Petros turned to Cassandra. "You are Maria's daughter?"

"Yes."

"You look just like your mother when she was a young girl."

Cassandra smiled.

Patting his great-grandson on the head, Petros said, "You can go now, Peppi."

Peppi gave Petros a hug, then smiling at Tony and Cassandra, ran out the open door into the bright sunlight.

Petros pointed to three wooden chairs. "Please, have a seat."

Tony, Cassandra and Petros sat down in the old chairs.

"You speak English very well," Tony said.

"When I was very young, my mother was… What's the word for someone who takes care of another person's children?"

"You mean 'governess'?" Tony replied.

"Yes. Governess. That's it." Petros continued. "My mother was the governess for a British family. She worked for them for over twelve years. She always told me that I must learn English."

"She taught you well," Tony said.

"Yes, she also opened the world of books to me. I read many books." Petros paused, thinking. "Hemingway was my favorite. I loved 'The Old Man and the Sea'."

"That was a good one," Tony agreed.

"Yes. And now… I am that old man." Petros sighed, looking off in the distance. Turning back to Tony, he asked, "Tell me, Tony, why have you come to Tibius?"

"To find some answers." Tony said.

Petros studied him carefully. "What is it that you want to know?"

"Cassandra's parents grew up here."

"Yes, I knew them well," Petros said. "I was very fond of Maria."

"And Nikos?"

A shadow passed over Petros' face. "He was a good boy. Then something happened. He changed."

Cassandra sat up straight in her chair.

"In what way?" Tony asked.

"He was never satisfied with the life here. He wanted more. He started going to the harbor. Seeing the big boats and all the rich people made him envious."

Cassandra and Tony listened intently.

"Nikos was determined to make money." Petros paused. "He swore that he would never be like his father, who was never successful at anything. Nikos knew that one day… he would be rich." Petros turned to Cassandra. "Did he get his wish?"

"Yes," Cassandra said, nodding.

Tony thought for a moment, then asked, "Petros, why did you send Peppi to bring us to you?"

"I have something that I must tell you… something that I have never told anyone before. I have been praying that you would come in time."

Tony and Cassandra looked at Petros, questioningly.

"It's my heart," Petros said, raising his hand to his chest. "The doctors told me that I do not have much longer to live."

Tony thought back to what Katrina had told him: *The answer is there… in Greece… but it won't be for much longer.*

"Before I die, there is something I must tell you," Petros said.

Tony listened, alert.

"I am a fisherman. I have been one for my entire life. When I was younger, I used to fish at night, when the other fishermen had gone home."

He looked at both Cassandra and Tony.

"I was there the night of the sacrifice."

"Sacrifice?" Tony asked, remembering the folded printout in his pocket.

"Yes. I was fishing. My boat was only fifty meters from the cove. At first, I only saw the light from the torches. Then, as the men drew nearer, I heard the chanting."

Cassandra was beginning to look pale, a light sweat breaking out on her forehead. She began to have trouble breathing.

"There had been rumors of a strange cult, but no one had ever seen them before." Petros paused, a mixture of conflict and guilt upon his face. "I was going to row away, to go back home, but I did not. I lifted my oars into my boat and stayed where I was. The young men were so absorbed in what they were doing that no one noticed me. I did not realize the purpose of their mission at first, but then I heard the screams of the young boy. I saw what they were doing. I watched as they put him in the wet sand and buried him up to his neck."

Cassandra started gasping for air. She flashed back to her first visit with Father George and recalled how she felt as if she were drowning. *That's exactly what I was feeling*, Cassandra thought to herself.

Tony looked at Cassandra. "Are you okay?"

"I think so."

"You want some air," Tony asked.

"No, I'll be alright."

"Perhaps it's better that she doesn't hear what I have to say," Petros suggested to Tony.

"No!" Cassandra said, adamantly. "I want to hear."

Petros looked at Tony.

Tony nodded for him to go on.

Petros continued. "Deep in my heart, I was afraid. I wanted to stop them. I wanted to save the boy." His eyes began to fill with tears. "But there were twelve, strong young men and I was over seventy years old. I did nothing to stop their terrible deed. I could hear the screams of the boy as they buried him in the sand. His screams grew louder and louder, filled with terror. Then the waves started coming in, rushing in over his head."

Tony and Cassandra sat perfectly still listening to his every word.

"With pain in my heart I heard the boy's screams and did nothing. And then there was silence. The screams had stopped. There was only the sound of the sea. After a short while, the chanting began again. I quietly rowed away."

"How can something like that happen without anyone finding out?" Tony asked.

"Everyone in Telenos had heard about the cult, but no one had ever seen evidence of it before," Petros said.

"There is something I must show you," Petros said, getting up from his chair. Walking slowly over to a small desk, he opened a drawer. "I had a nephew who had been a member of the cult. He confessed to me after the sacrifice. He told me that he hadn't wanted to participate in the ceremony, but was too frightened to try to stop it." Petros retrieved a faded envelope from the desk drawer. Walking back to his chair, he sat down.

"After the sacrifice, my nephew quit the cult. A few days later, his fishing boat was found empty, not far from shore. His body was never found."

"That's terrible," Tony said.

Petros opened the faded envelope and withdrew the same gold ring that Cassandra had found in her father's drawer.

Cassandra gasped. "My father has the same ring."

"I know," Petros said. "My nephew told me that everyone who had participated in the sacrifice received one."

Tony leaned forward in his chair. "But how do you know that Nikos was one of them?"

"I could see their faces in the light from the torches." Petros paused. "Nikos was one of them."

"You mean my father killed the boy?" Cassandra asked,

leaning forward, her body tense.

"No. He didn't participate in the actual sacrifice. He just watched... as did I."

"Why didn't he try to stop it?" Cassandra asked.

"They would have killed him had he interfered."

Cassandra thought for a moment, her face serious. "But he could have tried to do *something*."

"So could I have," Petros said. "But I did nothing."

The ringing of Tony's cell phone sounded loud in the small room. Looking at the caller I.D., he said. "It's Mikéli." Speaking into his phone, Tony asked, "Where are you?" He listened. "Where do you want us to meet you?" Listening for a moment, he said, "Okay. See you there." Ending the call, Tony looked at Cassandra. "He wants us to meet him at Alexio's store in about fifteen minutes."

Cassandra nodded.

Tony turned to Petros. "I was going to ask you... why didn't you tell Father Mikéli what you just told us? After all, he is a priest."

"Yes," Petros said, "but he is also Maria's brother."

Tony nodded. "Petros, I'm curious about one more thing."

"Yes?" Petros asked.

"The sacrifice... what was it for?"

"It was a sacrifice to Apollo," Petros said, in a quiet voice.

There was an audible gasp from Cassandra.

Tony leaned forward in his chair, fascinated. "Has this been going on for a long time?" Tony asked.

"For as long as I can remember. Not the sacrifices," Petros clarified, "but the cult itself. The men are always young and poor. They are lured into the circle of believers with promises of riches and success."

"And they believe in Apollo?" Tony asked.

"Most of them don't. They just want the material things that the cult can bring them."

"What about Nikos? Do you think that he believes in Apollo?"

"I doubt it," Petros said. "He is much too cynical. I'm sure that he did it because he wanted money and power."

Tony thought for a moment, then asked, "Does this cult have a leader?"

"Yes... a man named Frank Stavros."

"That's my father's boss," Cassandra said, her voice shaky.

Petros nodded.

"But why would Stavros do it?" Tony asked. "He seems like the kind of man who has always had wealth."

"He has. But he is obsessed with power. And he believed that his means of obtaining it was through the worship of Apollo. You see, about twenty years ago, the fishing industry in Telenos was doing terribly and tourism had fallen off, too. At that time, Stavros took over as the leader of the cult. After the sacrifice, the fishing got much better and tourism started to boom."

"Interesting," Tony said.

"Most people would say that it was just a coincidence, but Stavros was convinced that it was due to Apollo."

"But why did they sacrifice a boy? I've read that Apollo

didn't want human sacrifices."

"I'm sure that it was Stavros' idea," Petros said. "He had the men do it in order to made sure that they would always stay loyal to him. It's very much like a deal with the Devil. You get what you want… but then you owe him your soul."

Chapter Fourteen

THE LIST

Mikéli, Cassandra and Tony sat down at the old wooden table in Mikéli's office. A tray, laden with fruit, cheese and bread, had already been placed there for them by one of the monks. There were also two opened bottles of Coca Cola and a pitcher of water.

"I'll have to thank the brothers in the kitchen later. I told them that we wouldn't be back in time for dinner. They seem to have thought of everything," Mikéli said, handing the Cokes to Tony and Cassandra. "I got an email from your mother earlier today," he said, turning to Cassandra. "She needs to hear from you. After you've finished eating, you can use my computer to write back to her. She's worried about you."

"I know," Cassandra said, picking at her food. "Uncle Mikéli?" she asked.

"Yes, Cassandra?"

"I'm not that hungry. Can I email Mom now?"

"Of course. The computer's right next door." Turning to Tony, Mikéli said, "I'll be right back."

After getting Cassandra settled at the computer, Mikéli returned to his office and sat down across from Tony.

"What's the matter with Cassandra?" Mikéli asked. "She seems upset about something."

"It's because of what happened at Petros'," Tony replied. "He told us about the sacrifice."

"The sacrifice?"

"Yes, the young boy. Sixteen years ago… the one who disappeared from the orphanage." Reaching into his back pocket, Tony retrieved the printout of the article about the missing boy. Handing it to Mikéli, he asked, "Hadn't you heard about it?"

Mikéli skimmed the article, then looked up at Tony. "There were rumors… ."

Reaching into his other pocket, Tony pulled out the faded envelope that Petros had given him. "Here," he said, handing it to Mikéli. "Petros wanted me to give this to you."

Opening the envelope, Mikéli retrieved the ring and a smaller envelope. He placed the small envelope on the table.

"Where did Petros get this?" Mikéli asked, holding the

ring in his hand.

"From his nephew."

Mikéli looked at Tony. "Petros' nephew disappeared many years ago. His fishing boat was found empty about a hundred meters offshore."

"I know," Tony said. "Petros told me. His nephew was a member of the cult."

"What cult?"

"The cult of Apollo."

Mikéli looked at Tony.

"He had given the ring to Petros in case anything happened to him," Tony said.

"Why didn't Petros tell me about any of this?" Mikéli asked, placing the ring on the table.

Reaching over, Tony picked up the smaller envelope and handed it to Mikéli.

"Open it," Tony said.

Carefully opening the envelope, Mikéli withdrew a folded piece of paper. Spreading it out on the table, he saw a list of twelve names. He started reading, stopping at the eighth name. "Nikos Theopoulos," he said aloud, a stunned look on his face.

"Yes. Nikos was one of them," Tony said. "He wasn't one of the men who actually performed the sacrifice, but he did participate in the ceremony."

"Does Cassandra know all this?" Mikéli asked.

"Yes. She was there when Petros talked about it." Tony paused. "She's upset because her father stood by and did nothing to stop it."

Mikéli thought for a moment. "She's very wise for her

age. It reminds me of a famous quote by an eighteenth century Irish philosopher: 'All that is necessary for evil to triumph is for good men to do nothing'."

Tony nodded. "That's exactly why she's so upset."

"Does Maria know anything about this?"

"I doubt it."

"There's one more name you should know about, but it's not on the list," Tony said.

"Who is it?"

"Frank Stavros."

"That's Nikos' boss," Mikéli said. "Was he there, too?"

"No. But he's the leader of the cult. Petros said that he's the only one who really believes in Apollo." Tony started to say something, then stopped.

"What is it, Tony?" Mikéli asked. "You look as though you wanted to say something, but stopped yourself."

"It's about Apollo," Tony said. "I was wondering..."

"Go on," Mikéli said.

"I think that the sacrifice might have awakened Apollo."

Mikéli leaned forward on his elbows. "And what makes you think that Apollo has been 'awakened'?"

"Has Maria told you anything about Cassandra's precognition?"

"Yes."

"When you were in seminary, did you study any mythology?" Tony asked.

"Not in seminary, but in college I did."

"Then you know about the myth of Cassandra."

"Of course."

"Then what I'm about to say shouldn't come as a surprise."

Mikéli looked at Tony.

"When Nikos joined the cult," Tony continued, "he wanted money and power. He knew that he would have to give up his soul in return for those things."

Mikéli nodded.

"The one thing he hadn't counted on was that once Apollo had been awakened, instead of Nikos' soul as payment, Apollo would want Cassandra."

Mikéli was silent. He leaned back in his chair, deep in thought. After a few moments, he said, "You really believe this, don't you Tony?"

"Yes."

"But how did you know what to look for?"

"I didn't. Katrina told me."

"Who's Katrina?"

"She's a psychic. She told me that I had to come to Greece. When I saw the article about the missing boy, I knew we had to come to Telenos."

The gentle ringing of church bells announced the start of evening vespers. "I have to go to vespers," Mikéli said, getting up from his chair. He walked toward the door. "I'll be back in a little while."

"I'll go check on Cassandra," Tony said. As he got up from his chair, he felt his cell phone vibrate. Reaching into his pocket, he retrieved the phone. A text message from Katrina was on the display:

> Don't let Cassandra out of your sight.
> Come home as soon as you can.
> It is not safe for her there.

Tony quickly typed the words: 'Will do', and sent the reply back to Katrina. He headed straight for the computer room.

* * *

Cassandra was standing motionless at the small window in the computer room.

"Cassandra?" Tony asked.

She seemed not to hear him.

"Cassandra?" Tony said, a little louder.

Cassandra turned to face Tony. There was a blank look in her eyes.

"Did you finish emailing your mother?"

"Yes," she said, her voice flat, lifeless.

"What were you looking at?" Tony asked, approaching the window.

"Nothing," Cassandra said, again in the same emotionless voice.

Looking over Cassandra's shoulder, Tony saw an island in the distance. "Mikéli's gone to vespers," he said. "He said he'd be back in a little while. We can wait in his office."

"No," Cassandra said. "I want to go to bed. I'm tired."

"Alright. I'll see you to your room."

Tony and Cassandra walked down the hallway together. Opening the door to her room, Cassandra stepped inside.

"Are you all right?" Tony asked, concerned.

"Yes," Cassandra said, in the same flat voice.

"I'll be with Mikéli in his office if you need me."

Cassandra nodded and closed the door.

Tony stood outside her room, a worried look on his

face.

*   *   *

Tony walked over to the window in Mikéli's office. He looked out the small window at the island that Cassandra had been looking at. A feeling of uneasiness came over him.

"Where's Cassandra?" Tony heard Mikéli ask.

Tony turned to see Mikéli enter the office. "She was tired," Tony replied. "She went to bed." Tony looked back out the window. "Mikéli? What's that island over there?"

Walking over to where Tony was standing, Mikéli looked out the window. "That's Delos. Legend has it that it's the birthplace of Apollo."

~ Cassandra ~

Chapter Fifteen
THE PATH

Cassandra awakened, slowly opening her eyes.

"Cassandra," a voice called, as if from far away.

"Tony?" she said aloud, turning on the light in her room. There was no answer. Having fallen asleep in her clothes, Cassandra got up from the bed and stepped out into the hall.

"Cassandra," the voice called again, this time stronger, more commanding.

Unable to resist the alluring voice, Cassandra walked, as if mesmerized, down the hall toward the exit door. Opening the door, she stepped out into the evening air. A warm breeze was blowing.

"Cassandra," the voice called again.

"Tony?" she called out. There was no response. In the distance, Cassandra noticed the strange island. She felt a pulling, as though she were being drawn in that direction.

The sun had already set, but the sky was still light. Cassandra began walking toward the edge of the cliff.

*   *   *

Tony woke up in a cold sweat. He looked around, getting his bearings. "Cassandra," he said aloud, sensing that something was wrong. Turning on the light, he quickly got dressed and ran down the hall to Cassandra's room. The door was open. The light was on. Her bed was empty. Tony panicked. Running to the window, he looked out. He was horrified to see Cassandra standing at the edge of the cliff.

"No! Don't!" Tony yelled. He tried to open the small window, but it was stuck. He turned and ran out of the room, down the hall, and out the exit door. He ran to where he last saw Cassandra standing. She was not there. "No-o-o-o!" he yelled.

Overcome by a sense of dread, he looked over the edge of the cliff. Seeing the waves crashing onto the rocks hundreds of feet below, Tony felt nauseous.

"Oh, God. Please let her be alive," Tony said aloud, knowing in his heart that no one could survive such a fall.

Suddenly Tony noticed three small steps carved into the cliff. He ran over to them. The steps led to a path that had been carved out of the side of the cliff. Wide enough for one person, it seemed to lead down the face of the cliff to the sea below.

Cautiously, Tony took his first step. The dust on the rocky path made the going treacherous. He moved carefully along the footpath, grabbing onto the rough face of the cliff wherever possible. Step by step, he made his way along the path down the side of the precipice.

The wind had picked up. The sound of the waves crashing on the rocks below traveled up the side of the cliff. Tony resumed his descent down the narrow path. The wind seemed to be blowing stronger, almost as if it were directed at Tony, trying to make him fall. Tony stopped for a moment, grabbing onto the side of the cliff. After a few moments, the wind died down. He continued making his way down the path.

Suddenly, he caught his breath. Lying motionless in a clump of bushes growing out of the side of the cliff, Tony saw Cassandra.

"Cassandra!" Tony called to her, trying to get closer to where she was snared in the dry bushes. Leaning over, he gently touched her arm. Cassandra moaned slightly.

"You're alive," Tony said, his voice choked with emotion.

Opening her eyes, Cassandra saw Tony. The bushes began to crackle from her slight movements.

"Tony," Cassandra whispered, barely able to speak.

"Careful. Don't move. I've got to get you back on solid ground." Putting his arm around Cassandra's waist, Tony tried to lift her off of the bush. Losing his balance, he was forced to let go of her. The bushes crackled under her weight.

Tony glanced down at the rocks below. "Oh, God, give me the strength to save her," Tony prayed under his breath. Getting a firm grip on a hole in the cliff wall, he reached around Cassandra's waist. This time, with a more secure grip on the cliff wall, he managed to lift her off of the bushes.

"Are you hurt?" he asked, gently laying her down on the path.

"I'm not sure," she answered, her voice barely above a whisper.

"Do you think you can stand?" Tony asked.

"I don't know."

"Here, let me help you," he said, putting his arm around Cassandra. "Put your arm around my neck," he instructed her.

With Tony's help, Cassandra managed to get to her feet.

"What do you think?" he asked.

"I think I'm okay," she said, her voice a little stronger.

"Do you think you'll be able to walk?"

"I'm not sure," she replied. "I'll try." Tentatively, she took a step. "I can do it."

"Okay. Let's go. We've got to get back to solid ground. The path's only wide enough for one person. I'll lead the way."

Holding onto the rough surface of the cliff with his left hand, Tony put his right hand behind his back. "Hold onto my hand," he said.

Tony and Cassandra slowly made their way up the narrow path toward the top of the cliff. At the end of the path, Tony stepped up onto level ground, Cassandra following closely behind him, still holding tightly onto his hand.

They both stood still for a moment as the reality of what they had just survived began to sink in.

"How did you know where to look for me?" Cassandra asked.

"Something woke me up. I saw you standing by the edge of the cliff. I thought you were going to jump."

"I wouldn't do that."

"Then why were you out there?"

"Someone was calling me. I thought it was you."

"It wasn't me. I was asleep."

"You weren't calling me?"

"No."

"Then it was *him*."

Tony stared at her, then looked toward the island of Delos, still visible in the fading light.

"I heard his voice once before. I didn't know what it was. It makes perfect sense now."

"What do you mean?" Tony asked.

"Because of my father… the cult… the whole thing."

"That's why I thought you had jumped. Not just because you knew about your father, but because of everything that's been going on."

"No. I'd never do that. But now I know for sure who was calling me. It was Apollo. He didn't get the first Cassandra… and now he wants me."

"I won't let him have you," Tony said, putting his arms around her.

"Tony, if it weren't for you, I'd be dead," Cassandra said, looking into Tony's eyes.

Tony drew her close. "When I thought I'd lost you… when I thought you had jumped… it was like my whole world had ended."

Cassandra started to cry. "I love you, Tony."

"I love you, too," Tony said, wiping away one of her tears. "More than you can even begin to imagine."

Cassandra raised her face to his, her cheeks still wet with tears. Tony leaned down and gently touched his lips to hers.

In the distance, a low rumble of thunder could be heard.

Reluctantly, they pulled apart.

"I'd better get you back inside," Tony said, looking over his shoulder at Delos.

Arms around each other, Tony and Cassandra walked slowly back to the monastery.

End of Book One

Book Two

CASSANDRA

&

The Lost City of Troy

~SP~
Studio Publishing

Acknowledgments

"Brian" - a.k.a., Dr. C. Brian Rose, James B. Pritchard Professor of Archaeology, University of Pennsylvania; Curator-in-Charge, Mediterranean Section, Penn Museum of Archaeology and Anthropology.

Thank you for your patience and kindness and for always being there to answer any and all of our questions.

Love is composed of a single soul inhabiting two bodies.

Aristotle (384 B.C. – 322 B.C.)

~ Cassandra ~

Chapter Sixteen

LAST RITES

Telenos, Greece

From the moment that Tony and Cassandra stepped across the threshold into the monastery, they sensed that something was wrong. The lights, which before had been lowered to the point where they were emitting a gentle golden glow, were now fully turned on, filling the hallway with a harsh white light.

There was a commotion in the hallway. A young monk, wearing a coarse brown robe and leather sandals, hurried toward Tony and Cassandra, a look of concern on his face.

"What's going on?" Tony asked.

"We got a call from Petros' son about half an hour ago," the young monk said. "Petros is dying and wanted Father Mikéli to perform last rites."

Suddenly, Mikéli appeared in the main entrance to the monastery. He said something to two of the monks, after which they hurried off to the chapel. Moments later, the sound of a lone church bell ringing could be heard, not only in the monastery, but also throughout the surrounding countryside.

Tony and Cassandra walked over to Mikéli, who seemed to be coordinating the activities of the other monks.

"What happened?" Cassandra asked.

"Petros died. He is now with our heavenly Father," Mikéli answered.

Tears began to fill Cassandra's eyes. "But we were just there. We were with him less than four hours ago. He seemed fine."

"No, honey, he wasn't," Mikéli said, gently. "He was very ill. His son told me that Petros' doctor had told him that he didn't have long to live, but Petros kept holding on, waiting for something... he didn't know for what. And then the both of you came."

"Oh, God," Cassandra said, no longer able to hold back the tears, which were flowing freely down her cheeks. "It's our fault. We never should have gone to see him."

"On the contrary," Mikéli said. "Petros told me to tell you that God had answered his prayers by sending you and Tony to him. He said that after he told you his story, an enormous weight had been lifted from his shoulders and that he was ready for his journey home." Mikéli paused, taking a handkerchief from his pocket and handing it to Cassandra. "He also wanted me to tell you not to be sad… that if you hadn't come, he would have had to die, taking his terrible secret with him. This way he felt that he could go in peace."

Cassandra's crying subsided slightly. She wiped away a few tears with the handkerchief.

"It's just like Katrina told me," Tony said, turning to Cassandra.

Cassandra gave him a puzzled look, not fully understanding.

"I have to go," Mikéli said, turning to join some of the monks who were standing, waiting at the end of the hall. "Oh, Cassandra… you and Tony had better make arrangements to get back home as soon as possible. Your mother emailed me saying that your father was in a rage… and that you had to come home right away. You'd better go and email her." Mikéli turned and started to walk away. Looking over his shoulder at Cassandra, he said, "I'll see you in a little while."

* * *

Cassandra sat in front of the old fashioned desktop computer that rested on the table in the computer room of the monastery. She opened her email account and read her mother's email.

"What'd she say?" Tony asked.

"She said that Dad is furious. He said that he never would have let me leave the country if I had been staying with him. He's going to use all of this against her in the custody hearing." Cassandra continued reading. "I'll have to write her back." She started typing, then stopped and turned to look at Tony. "What did you mean by… 'It's just like Katrina said?'"

"Do you remember when I called you and said I that had to go to Greece right away?"

Cassandra nodded.

"Well, when I went to see her, her trance took her back to the same scene that she had seen when she was holding your father's ring… the exact same scene that Petros described. She came out of the trance abruptly and said, 'Tony… you've got to go to Greece right away.' When I asked her what she meant, she said, 'The answer is there in Greece… but it won't be for much longer.' Then she said, 'If you don't get the answer now, it may be lost forever.'"

"How could she have known about Petros?"

"She didn't," Tony answered. "She just had this sense of urgency."

"But how could she go into a trance? You didn't have my father's ring with you."

"Remember those old Greek coins that your father had given to my dad for his birthday a few years ago."

"Sort of," Cassandra said, trying to remember.

"The coins were still in the original wrappers," Tony continued, "untouched by anyone but your father. I brought them with me to Katrina… and she was able to use them. And…" Tony hesitated for a moment.

"What is it? You started to say something."

"She did a reading on me," Tony said, looking somewhat embarrassed.

"What did she see?" Cassandra asked, interested.

"That I was in love with you."

Cassandra blushed. "That's what she learned from the reading?"

"She didn't mean the present," Tony said. "She was talking about when you were in Troy... three thousand years ago. You had a brother, Helenus. He was my best friend... and I was in love with you."

Cassandra sat in stunned silence, trying to absorb what Tony had just told her.

"Look, I've got to use the computer," Tony said, breaking the silence. "I've got to book us a flight back to the States."

Getting up, Cassandra relinquished her seat to Tony. She walked a few feet away, a thoughtful look on her face.

Sitting down at the computer, Tony began to look up flights from Athens to New York.

"There's one that leaves tomorrow from Athens at three-thirty in the afternoon," he said. "We'll have to be on that nine-thirty commuter flight from here to Athens in the morning." Tony paused for a moment. "I'll book it right now."

"No, wait!" Cassandra said, walking back over to where Tony was sitting. "Don't book it."

"Why not?"

"Look up the flights from here to Troy."

"What are you talking about?"

"I've got to go to Troy," Cassandra said. "If we go back to the States, my dad will ground me and I'll never have a chance to go again."

Tony thought for a moment. "You're serious about this, aren't you?"

"Yes. I've got to get to Troy."

Chapter Seventeen

FLIGHT TO ISTANBUL

"Athens News," the operator answered. "How may I direct your call?"

"Mr. Petrarkos' office," Tony said.

"Mr. Petrarkos' office," a female voice answered.

"Hi, Tina. It's Tony."

"Hey, Tony. Where are you?" Tina responded, happy to hear Tony's voice.

"In Telenos. We're coming to Athens."

"Your uncle will be delighted to see you. When are you coming?"

"Tomorrow morning. Is he available to speak?"

"Hold on. I'll check."

"Tony!" Dan answered.

"Uncle Dan," Tony said, "we're coming to Athens to-morrow morning."

"Great! Can't wait to see you. What time is your plane to New York?"

"We're not going to New York. We have to catch a flight to Istanbul."

"Istanbul? Why on earth are you going there?"

"Cassandra wants to go to Troy."

"Troy?" Tony could hear the concern in his uncle's voice.

"Yes," Tony answered. "I've made all the arrange-ments."

"You didn't answer my question," Dan continued. "Why are you going to Troy? There's nothing there but some old ruins."

"It's a long story, Uncle Dan. I don't have time to go into it right now."

"I'm completely against it, Tony," Dan said.

"You don't understand, Uncle Dan. We have to go. I've checked it all out on the computer"

"What are your plans?" Dan asked.

"I've booked a flight on Turkish Airways and a bed and breakfast place just outside of Çanakkale," Tony said. "It's only thirty-five dollars a night."

"I don't think that's such a good idea," Dan said. "Tony, maybe you and Cassandra should just forget about going to Troy and stay here with us for the night. We'll give you a nice homemade dinner before you head back home."

"You don't understand, Uncle Dan. Cassandra's set on going to Troy. If I don't go with her, she'll go by herself."

Dan was silent for a moment. "That's unacceptable. Let me make a few calls. I'll call you back in ten minutes. Okay?"

"Sure. Talk to you later." Tony ended the call on his cell phone. Leaving the room, Tony walked down the hall and knocked on the door to Cassandra's room.

"Yes?"

"It's me."

Cassandra immediately opened the door.

Tony noticed the opened suitcase on her bed.

"I'm all packed," Cassandra said. "What's happening?"

"I spoke with Uncle Dan. He's not thrilled about us going to Istanbul, but I told him that we're going. He's also not very happy with the travel arrangements I made."

Just then, Tony's cell phone hummed in his pocket. He looked at the caller I.D. and swiped his finger across the display.

"Hi, Uncle Dan."

"Tony, your father's going to kill me, but here's what I've arranged for you guys. Do you have something to write with?"

Tony took a note pad and pen out of his pocket. "Go ahead. I'm ready."

"I have you booked on Air France flight KL 1576. It departs Athens at 10:35 AM. It takes about an hour."

"Air France? That's an expensive flight."

"Tina's brother works for them. He was able to get me

a discount."

Tony started to object. "Uncle Dan, I can't let you...."

"Tony," Dan interrupted. "Let me handle this. I know what I'm doing."

Tony sighed. "Alright."

Dan continued, "When you land in Istanbul, a fellow named Ishtak will meet you at the gate and take you to the other end of the airport, where you'll have to catch a connecting flight to the airport in Çanakkale. From there, you can take a taxi to the Grand Hotel, where I've booked you and Cassandra adjoining rooms."

"The Grand Hotel!" Tony exclaimed. "That's a four-star hotel, Uncle Dan. We can't afford that."

"Don't worry about it. It's covered. The manager's a friend of mine and I got a good rate.

"But even with a discount it's a lot of money," Tony protested.

"Don't be misled by the name. It's more like a three-story Holiday Inn than any kind of 'Grand Hotel'. Besides, it's worth it to me to know that you're both in a safe place and that you each have your privacy." Dan paused a moment, then continued. "Lastly, I've got you booked on a flight back to the States. Delta Airlines, Flight 73, departing Istanbul at 12:15 PM. You've got to catch the Wednesday morning commuter flight from Çanakkale to Istanbul. If you miss that flight to Istanbul, you'll have to stay an extra two days because they only fly in and out of Çanakkale three days a week. Your folks are worried sick and so is Cassandra's mother." Dan paused. "I know I can count on you, Tony."

"How am I ever going to thank you, Uncle Dan?"

"No need to. That's what family is for. Just promise me that you'll take good care of Cassandra… and that the both of you will come back safe and sound."

"I promise. Thanks, Uncle Dan," Tony said, ending the call.

"What was all that about?" Cassandra asked. "I heard you say something about a four-star hotel."

"Uncle Dan's booked us adjoining rooms at one of the nicest hotels in Çanakkale."

"What's Çanakkale?" Cassandra asked.

"It's the nearest major town to Troy," Tony said. "It's where most of the tours leave from."

"How can we afford it?" Cassandra asked. "We barely had enough money to get here."

"He's paying for it… and for the flight home, too."

Cassandra was quiet for a moment. "We'll have to pay him back."

"I know," Tony said. "Look, I'd better get packed. We have to catch that early morning flight out of here to Athens." Tony turned and started to leave the room.

"Wait!" Cassandra said. "What'll we tell Mikéli? We can't tell him that we're going to Troy. He'd never let us go." She paused a moment. "But I also don't want to lie to him. What'll we say?"

"We'll tell him that we're leaving for Athens in the morning and that we should be home in a couple of days."

Cassandra had a skeptical look on her face.

"It's not a lie," Tony said. "We *are* going to Athens.

That's where we're catching the connecting flight to Istanbul."

Cassandra bit her lower lip. "I have a feeling that he's not going to buy it."

* * *

The air was surprisingly warm as Tony and Cassandra, pulling their suitcases behind them, headed for the small taxi that was waiting outside the courtyard gate of the monastery. Though the sun had not yet risen, the sky was light enough for Tony to see the island of Delos in the distance.

"Airport, yes?" the cab driver asked in his broken English.

"Yes," Tony said, as he and Cassandra started to climb into the back seat of the taxi.

"Hey! You can't leave without letting me have my goodbye hug," Mikéli called to them, hurrying out to the cab.

"We didn't want to wake you," Tony said, as Cassandra set her bag down in order to hug her uncle.

"I get to see my niece once every ten years and you guys are worried about me getting a few extra minutes of sleep?" Cassandra's eyes filled with tears as she hugged her uncle goodbye. Tony extended his right hand to Mikéli. "What's this handshake stuff?" Mikéli asked, letting go of Cassandra and opening his arms to give Tony a hug. "I can't believe it's been only twenty-four hours. You've become like a son to me."

Tony returned Mikéli's hug, surprised that he was beginning to feel so choked up. He was finding it hard to speak.

Standing back from Tony, Mikéli said, "I know that Cassandra will be in good hands with you." Turning to Cassandra, Mikéli said, "Call me when you get to Athens."

Cassandra nodded. "I will."

Placing the suitcases on the seat next to the driver, Tony climbed into the back of the taxi. Cassandra turned to give Mikéli one last hug, then quickly got into the cab before her uncle could see her tears.

Rolling down the windows of the taxi, Tony and Cassandra waved to Mikéli, who's image grew smaller and smaller in the distance as the cab made its way down the dusty, winding road that led away from St. Ignatius' Monastery. Cassandra's tears were flowing freely now.

As the cab rounded a bend in the road, Tony caught a glimpse of the island of Delos, which was now shimmering in the early morning sunlight. He felt almost as though the island were mocking him. *That's ridiculous*, he thought. Yet he couldn't shake the feeling. A chill ran up his spine. Tony knew that it was not over. Moving closer to Cassandra, he put his arm protectively around her. Looking at Delos one last time, he swore, half under his breath, "I won't let you have her."

~ Cassandra ~

Chapter Eighteen
ÇANAKKALE, TURKEY

The commuter plane taxied up to a small, but modern one-story building that was the terminal for the Çanakkale Airport. Cassandra watched through her window as several men pushed a rolling set of boarding stairs toward the exit door of the plane. The sound of latches being undone could be heard as the steward opened the exit door to the boarding stairs.

"Thank you for flying Turkish Airways," the steward announced over the intercom. "We hope you enjoyed the flight. Kindly remember to remove all of your personal items from the storage compartments."

Baggage in hand, Tony and Cassandra walked toward the front of the plane and out onto the boarding stairs. The afternoon sun was much hotter than either of them had anticipated.

Tony and Cassandra walked down the stairs and onto the tarmac.

"Do you need any help with that?" Tony asked, indicating Cassandra's suitcase.

"No, I can handle it."

The two of them hurried toward the terminal, hoping that it was air-conditioned. Once inside the cool building, they waited a few minutes before stepping back outside into the humid heat to hail a taxi.

*   *   *

Climbing into the back seat of the cab, Tony and Cassandra were pleasantly surprised by the fact that it, too, was air-conditioned. The driver turned around, a questioning expression on his face. "Otel?"

"Yes, the Grand Hotel, please," Tony answered.

Turning on the meter, which was mounted on the dashboard, the driver pulled away from the terminal building. Moments later they were on a modern, four-lane highway. After about ten minutes, the driver turned onto a local road.

"There are so many apartment buildings," Cassandra commented, surprised. "I thought it was going to be a sleepy little town."

"I did, too," Tony said.

A worried expression passed over Cassandra's face. "Mikéli asked me to call him from the Athens Airport."

"We didn't have time," Tony reminded her. "We barely had time to catch the plane to Istanbul"

"He'll be worried," Cassandra said.

At that moment, Tony's cell phone rang. He looked at the caller I.D. "It's Mikéli!"

Cassandra gasped.

Tony answered the call. "Hey, Mikéli. What's up?"

"How do like Çanakkale?"

Tony, nearly dropping his phone, turned to Cassandra. "He knows we're here!"

Cassandra eyes got big.

"How did you know we were here?" Tony asked.

"You'd make a terrible spy. You left your entire travel research in the history of the browser on my computer."

"Oh," Tony said, feeling a little foolish.

"Look," Mikéli said, anticipating that Cassandra would think that he was angry with them, "tell Cassandra that I'm not angry. I had a feeling that you guys were up to something."

"We're going home as soon as we finish here," Tony said.

"Tony, all I care about is that you take care of Cassandra and that you guys get home safely."

"Thanks, Mikéli."

"By the way," Mikéli said, "you never told me why you're in Çanakkale."

"We have to go Troy."

Mikéli was silent for a moment, then said, "That makes perfect sense." He continued, a note of concern in his voice. "Where will you be staying?"

"The Grand Hotel."

"That's a good hotel," Mikéli said, sounding relieved. "Look, I have to run. Talk to you later. Give my love to Cassandra."

"Okay. Bye." Tony ended the call and turned to Cassandra. "He's not mad at us."

Cassandra's whole body seemed to relax.

A few minutes later, the cab driver pulled into the circular driveway of the Grand Hotel.

* * *

Tony held the glass door for Cassandra. He followed her across the threshold, entering the lobby. He and Cassandra approached the front desk, where a smiling young woman in her mid-twenties stood behind the counter.

"Yes?" the clerk inquired.

"Tony Petrarkos."

The clerk looked at the display of one of the computers, which had been built into the front desk counter top. "Ah, Petrarkos," she said, looking up at Tony. Swiping two room-key cards through the card reader, the clerk placed the keys, each inside a small paper folder, and handed them to Tony. "Rooms 311 and 313. Enjoy your stay, Mr. Petrarkos." The clerk smiled, first at Tony, then at Cassandra. "That'll be the elevator on the right," she said, pointing toward the elevator.

As Tony and Cassandra started walking away from the desk, Cassandra remarked, "What about getting to Troy?"

"Oh… you're right," Tony said.

Turning around, they walked back to the front desk.

The clerk looked up as they approached.

"I heard that you have tour groups that go to Troy," Tony said to the clerk.

"Yes. They're two-day tours. The first day the group visits Gallipoli... the second day, Troy."

"We have to leave on Wednesday," Tony said. "Is there any way that we can just visit Troy?"

"I'm sorry, but the only English-speaking tour starts tomorrow," the clerk said. Thinking for a moment, she said, "Hold on a minute. Let me check something." The clerk looked down at the computer, then back up at Tony. "Parlez-vous français?" she asked.

"Un peu," Tony replied, surprised. "Why?"

"We have a French-speaking tour that left for Gallipoli this morning," the clerk said. "That means that they'll be leaving for Troy tomorrow. I see that there's room for two more on the bus."

"That would be perfect," Tony said.

"The van leaves the hotel promptly at 9:00 AM," the clerk said. "Please be here at the front desk a few minutes before that."

"Great. Can you program a wake-up call for room 311 at 8:00 AM ?"

"Of course," the clerk said, making a few keystrokes on the keyboard. "Will there be anything else, Mr. Petrarkos?"

"No, thank you," Tony answered.

"Enjoy your stay," the clerk said as Tony and Cassandra headed for the elevator.

Looking straight ahead as they waited for the elevator,

Cassandra said, "I didn't know that you spoke French."

"I don't."

"But you understood what she was saying."

"She just asked me if I spoke any French. I told her 'a little'."

"I'm impressed."

"Don't be," Tony said, as they stepped into the elevator pulling their suitcases behind them. "I can barely get by."

The elevator started its ascent to the third floor. Turning to Cassandra, Tony asked, "Do you mind that the tour is going to be in French?"

"Of course not," Cassandra said. "I just want to get there."

Chapter Nineteen

THE LOST CITY OF TROY

The ringing of the telephone sounded like a fire alarm, waking Tony from a deep sleep. Lurching forward, he fumbled for the phone on the end table next to his bed and quickly put the receiver to his ear.

"Hello?" Tony said into the phone. The line was dead. It took a few seconds before he realized that it was the automated wake-up call that he had requested the evening before. Putting the phone back in its cradle, Tony sat up on the edge of the bed for about thirty seconds until he was sure that he was fully awake. Getting up, he headed for the bathroom. After a quick shower, he got dressed, putting on his white polo shirt and khaki chinos.

Walking across the room to the door connecting his room to Cassandra's, he knocked gently. "Cassandra?" he asked, softly. Getting no response, he opened the door only to find Cassandra's bed empty. The door to her bathroom was closed. Hearing the sound of water running in the shower, Tony closed the door. Grabbing a pen and note pad, he jotted down a note and slipped it under Cassandra's door.

Meet you at the front desk... Tony

* * *

About ten minutes later, Cassandra, dressed in a white cotton summer dress and white sandals, stepped out of the elevator and into the lobby. Her long brown hair, still slightly damp, hung down over her shoulders. She walked over to where Tony was standing at a buffet table where they were serving coffee, juice and rolls.

"You're wearing a dress," he commented, trying to hide the affect that she was having on him.

"There was a tour brochure on my dresser," she said, pouring herself a small glass of orange juice. "It said that we'll be visiting some religious sites after Troy. Women aren't allowed to wear pants. It's some kind of religious law."

"I didn't know that," Tony said. "It's a good thing you brought a dress with you."

Cassandra nodded. "It's too hot for jeans anyway," she said, taking a sip of her orange juice.

"We haven't got much time," Tony said, gulping his coffee. "They're leaving in five minutes."

*   *   *

"Bonjour…. bonjour… bonjour," the Turkish guide repeated to each person as they boarded the Mercedes mini-bus.

Tony and Cassandra nodded as the guide greeted them. Working their way to the back of the mini-bus, they exchanged friendly smiles with the already seated members of the tour group. They sat down in the two vacant seats.

A woman with a friendly-looking face turned around and asked, "Êtes-vous d'Angleterre?"

"Non," Tony responded. "Nous sommes Américains."

The woman smiled and turned to face the front of the mini-bus.

"What did she say?" Cassandra asked.

"She asked if we were from England."

"What did you tell her?"

"I told her that we're American."

"Oh," Cassandra said. "Your French is much better than you said it was."

"Not really," Tony replied.

*   *   *

Tony and Cassandra sat looking out the windows of the mini-bus as it traveled along the modern four-lane highway. The relatively flat countryside appeared to be mostly farmland, golden in color from wheat crops. Occasional groves of neatly planted olive trees dotted the landscape.

The guide, nicknamed 'Maurice', for the sake of the French tourists, was standing at the front of the bus giving a brief history of Troy in French.

"Can you understand what he's saying?" Cassandra asked Tony.

"A little," Tony said. "He's talking about a guy named Schliemann, a German businessman, who came here just a little over a hundred years ago looking for the lost city of Troy."

"Why did they call it the lost city of Troy?"

"Because nobody believed that it actually existed. Schliemann came here and started digging. Everyone thought that it was just some legendary place… and that the Trojan War was just a story.

Cassandra listened, interested.

"Schliemann loved Homer's poetry. He believed that Homer was writing about a real city when he described it in the Iliad. "

Tony listened further as Maurice spoke.

"He says that Schliemann came looking for gold."

"Gold?"

"Yes, Schliemann believed that there were vast quantities of gold artifacts buried in Troy."

"And… did he find the gold?"

"From what I can understand, he did… but it wasn't from the right Troy."

"What do you mean?"

Tony continued. "Apparently, there were nine cities of Troy. Each time one was destroyed… another was built on top of it. Schliemann thought that he had found the city that Homer had described in the Iliad, but he had dug too deep. It was not the Troy of the Trojan War."

Cassandra looked deep in thought. "Which was *my* Troy?"

"I'm not sure. They think that the sixth city was the one during the Trojan War."

The mini-bus began to slow down. Tony caught a glimpse of a sign on the side of the highway, which read: Troya Tarihi Milli Parki. Below that, several translations appeared, one of which was in English.

"Troy Historical National Park," Tony said, half-aloud, as the bus made a right turn off the highway onto a two-lane blacktop road that headed in the direction of the park.

Cassandra was sitting straight up in her seat, alert. She looked out the window and saw some roadside souvenir stands tended by women dressed in traditional Turkish costumes. Hundreds of tiny plastic Trojan Horses and other memorabilia cluttered the tables. The women waved at the bus as it drove by.

The bus slowed down, turning left into a parking lot already filled with tour buses and taxicabs.

"It looks crowded," Cassandra said, glancing around.

Tony checked his watch. "It's only nine-thirty."

As Cassandra and Tony stepped out of the mini-bus and onto the parking lot, Cassandra looked up to see a large wooden horse jutting up into the sky.

"Oh, my gosh!" Cassandra exclaimed. "There it is."

As Tony and Cassandra approached the horse, they could see people milling around, taking pictures. Some were waving up at people who had climbed up into the wooden horse and were leaning out of open windows that had been built into the upper portion of the horse.

"That's not the *real* one, is it?" Cassandra asked.

"No way," Tony replied. "It looks brand new. They probably built it just for the tourists."

The sky was beginning to darken.

"Venez avec moi," Maurice said. He continued speaking in French for a few moments as he led the small group to the entrance gate designated for the pre-paid group tours of the park.

Tony turned to Cassandra. "He wants us to follow him. He said that if it starts to rain, the path will get too slippery and we'll have to stop the tour, so he wants to start right away."

Cassandra looked relieved, uninterested in the fake wooden horse. She was anxious to start the tour.

* * *

At each point of interest along the dirt path, Maurice droned on in French about some obscure archeological theory. After seeing several points of interest, the group moved forward onto what appeared to be a boardwalk-like wooden sidewalk, which made walking much easier.

The sky continued to darken. Maurice raised his hand and the group, once again came to a halt, gathering around a large pile of rocks. He resumed his memorized dialogue, talking about the ancient site.

Tony noticed that Cassandra's attention seemed to be elsewhere.

Maurice stopped talking and waved for the group to follow him. He led them past a small hill, pointing to an area that was littered with huge, broken pieces of columns, lying haphazardly in a grassy area. Pointing in the direction of the broken columns, he explained that this rubble was all that remained of the palace of King Priam and the royal family. The group continued along the path, walking past a roped-off stone road that led up to the grassy area where the pillars lay. Tony started to follow.

"No... wait!" Cassandra said, grabbing Tony's arm. Standing totally still, her head erect, her eyes alert, bright, she cocked her head as if listening for something.

Tony watched as Maurice and the group moved ahead, disappearing around a bend in the path. The sky was darkening, appearing as if it were about to rain.

"Come on," Cassandra said. Tugging on Tony's arm, she stepped over the low rope barrier onto the ancient stone roadway.

"We're not allowed here," Tony said, nearly tripping on the rope as Cassandra pulled him. He looked over his shoulder, hoping that no one was watching.

"This way," Cassandra said, pulling on Tony's arm. He was amazed at her strength. He had never seen her this determined before. Tony knew that it would be pointless to try to stop her.

"Here!" she said, stopping suddenly.

Just then, Tony heard the voice of a guide speaking loudly in German. A tour group was approaching near to where he and Cassandra where standing.

"Get down," Tony whispered, grabbing Cassandra's arm.

Cassandra and Tony ducked down behind a low wall

so as not to be discovered. Cassandra, noticing a small round stone lying on the ground, picked it up and held it in her hand. Her eyes began to slowly close.

Tony, seeing that the group had walked past them, leaned over to Cassandra and said in a low voice, "It's okay. We can stand up now."

Cassandra did not respond. Holding her by the elbow, Tony helped her to her feet. She slowly stood up, her eyes still closed.

Suddenly, Cassandra felt as if the whole world was melting around her. She held tightly onto Tony's arm, feeling as though she was about to faint. "Tony," she cried out.

"Cassandra?" Tony replied, a worried look on his face... but Cassandra could not hear him.

"Tony?" she called out... but he was no longer there. She heard voices and laughter. They seemed to be coming from far away, echoing as if she were in a tunnel. She felt herself sliding downward.

Within seconds, the ground felt solid again. Cassandra repeated, "Tony?" She opened her eyes. The sunlight was so brilliant that it temporarily blinded her. Raising her hand to block the glaring light, she looked around. The rubble of the ruins had disappeared. Before her stood a palace of beautiful white limestone. About twenty feet in front of her, a little girl was sitting at a marble table, her back to Cassandra. She was wearing a long white summer dress. Two boys in their early teens were 'play fighting' with wooden swords and small metal shields.

Cassandra felt a tugging at her arm. Looking down, she

saw a young boy about nine years old, with large brown eyes and dark hair, wearing a white linen tunic and leather sandals.

"Are you looking for someone?" the boy asked. The two teenage boys lowered their wooden swords for a moment, turning toward Cassandra in order to have a better look at her, then returned to their swordplay.

It took a moment… then it hit her. Cassandra knew where she was. Looking down into the dark brown eyes of the young boy, she said, "I'm… I'm looking for Cassandra."

"She's right over there," the boy said, pointing to the little girl sitting at the marble table.

"Cassandra," he called out. "There's someone to see you."

The little girl turned her head. "Someone to see *me?*" she asked, getting up from the bench and looking toward Cassandra.

Cassandra gasped. The little girl looked just like she did when she was about nine years old.

The little girl walked toward Cassandra. "I *knew* you'd come," she said, looking up at her. Taking Cassandra by the hand, little Cassandra led her back to the table where she had been sitting.

"How did you know?" Cassandra asked, sitting down on the bench next her.

"I had a dream," the little girl said, matter-of-factly. "I've been waiting for you."

Cassandra looked at the little girl. She felt an immediate bond with her, as though she had known her forever.

There was a sense of familiarity about the whole place. It was as though she'd been there before. Birds were chirping, playfully flitting about, occasionally landing on large painted vases which were filled with plants.

"What lovely flowers," Cassandra commented, looking at the beautiful white flowers that were spread across the marble table.

"They're lilacs," little Cassandra said. "Father gave them to me for my birthday. I'm going to be nine tomorrow," she said proudly. "I'm making a wreath out of them."

Cassandra watched the little girl's fingers as they deftly tied together the sprigs of lilac flowers, forming a lovely wreath.

"Are you coming tomorrow?" little Cassandra asked, jolting Cassandra back to the moment.

"Tomorrow?" Cassandra replied, confused.

"Yes, it's my birthday." The little girl paused for a moment. "Well, actually, it's *our* birthday," she said, indicating the boy who had been tugging on Cassandra's arm "That's Helenus. He's my twin brother. He's inviting Anthony, his best friend. I can invite someone, too. I want *you* to come." Little Cassandra stood up, holding the wreath in her hands. "Here, try this on," she said, placing the wreath on Cassandra's head. "It's a little too small," little Cassandra commented. "I'll make you one that fits. I'll give it to you when you come tomorrow."

"Cassandra! Helenus!" a woman's voice called from the steps of the palace. Cassandra turned to see a regal-looking woman, in her mid-thirties, wearing an elegant, floor-length, deep purple gown, embroidered with gold thread, standing at the entrance to the palace.

"Coming, Mother," little Cassandra called out, placing the lilac wreath on the table. "I've got to go," she said to Cassandra. "I'll see you tomorrow at my party."

"I'm sorry, Cassandra, but I won't be able to come to your birthday celebration. I have to go back home."

The little girl, unable to hide her disappointment, seemed about to cry.

"Listen," Cassandra said, a serious look on her face. "Before I go, there's something I have to tell you. It's very important."

Little Cassandra stared at her, questioningly.

"A terrible danger lies ahead," Cassandra said, looking into the little girl's eyes. "There's going to be a great battle between Greece and Troy. The Greek army is going to come in many ships. They are going to attack Troy and burn it to the ground."

Little Cassandra laughed. "That's impossible! Father would *never* let that happen. Here… come with me." Taking Cassandra by the hand, she led her to the edge of the palace wall. Stepping up onto a small marble bench, little Cassandra said, "Look!"

Beyond the citadel wall, Cassandra could see an enormous city, consisting of buildings and streets that extended as far as the eye could see. The streets were bustling with activity. Horses pulling carts filled with merchandise, stopped in front of merchant shops that lined the streets. There were homes of both mud-brick and wood. At the outer limits of the city, a mighty stone wall rose up from the earth, protecting the city from potential aggressors.

"See?" the little Cassandra said. "There's no way that anyone could attack us."

"You've got to believe me," Cassandra pleaded.

"Father will protect us." The little girl abruptly changed the subject. "Please try to come tomorrow."

"Hector... Paris... Helenus... Cassandra.... come... all of you," the woman called again, a note of annoyance in her voice. "Your father is waiting."

Little Cassandra climbed off the bench. "I've got to go," she said. Standing on tiptoe, she gave Cassandra a kiss on the cheek. "Please try to come tomorrow." Little Cassandra started to walk away then stopped. Turning back to Cassandra, she said, "I'll make you a wreath that fits."

"I...." Suddenly the voices began to echo again. Cassandra felt herself slipping downward as though she were on a water slide. Her ears filled with a whooshing sound.

"Cassandra?" She heard her name being called. "Cassandra?" It was Tony's voice.

Cassandra opened her eyes. All that she could see was stones and rubble. Gone was the blue sky... the beautiful palace. Little Cassandra and her brothers were nowhere to be seen. The sky was dark. It had begun to rain. A rumble of thunder could be heard in the distance.

"Are you okay?" Tony asked.

Cassandra stared at him.

"Are you okay?" Tony repeated.

"I think so," Cassandra said, her voice shaky.

"You scared me," Tony continued. "You seemed like you were far away. I called your name, but you didn't respond. It was as if you didn't hear me."

"I didn't," Cassandra said.

"Come on. We've got to go. They'll be wondering where we are." Seeing that Cassandra was unsteady on her feet, Tony held her securely by the elbow as they stepped over the rope barrier and back onto the main path.

"Wait!" Cassandra said, grabbing Tony's arm. She stopped and turned, looking back at the place where they had just been standing. The rain was coming down hard. The rocks looked cold and barren. *Could I have imagined the whole thing?*

"Come on," Tony said, gently. "We've got to go."

~ Cassandra ~

Chapter Twenty

THE RIDE BACK

An angry-looking Maurice, holding a large black umbrella, stood beside the Mercedes mini-bus, which idled behind him. "Dépêchez-vous! Hurry!" he called to Tony and Cassandra.

Holding their souvenir programs above their heads in a feeble attempt to shield themselves from the rain, Tony and Cassandra ran across the parking lot toward Maurice.

Opening the door, Maurice ushered them into the bus, following closely behind. He uttered something in French under his breath. Cassandra and Tony made their way back to their assigned seats.

"What did he say?" Cassandra asked.

"I don't know," Tony answered. "It was too fast for me to understand... but I have a feeling that he's not too happy with us."

Tony and Cassandra, their clothes completely drenched, settled back into their seats. Cassandra started shivering.

The French woman sitting in the seat in front of them reached down into a big souvenir shopping bag and pulled out a large white sweatshirt that she had purchased in the gift shop. Turning in her seat, she handed it to Cassandra. "S'il vous plaît... prenez-la."

"She's asking you to please take it," Tony said.

"Thank you," Cassandra said, shivering. The woman nodded. Cassandra quickly slipped the sweatshirt over her soaking wet dress. Across the front of the sweatshirt was printed: Project Troia.

"Better?" Tony asked.

"Much," she said. "Merci," Cassandra said to the woman, who smiled and turned to face the front of the bus.

"What happened back there?" Tony asked. "I couldn't get through to you."

"I was *there*," she whispered.

Tony stared at her. "What are you talking about?"

"I was *there*," Cassandra repeated, excitedly. "In Troy... back *then*. I saw Cassandra. She was about eight years old. And her brothers. And her mother. And there was this incredible palace. Oh, Tony... it was so beautiful."

"Go on," Tony said, interested.

"It all happened so quickly. I was sitting next to her. Cassandra was weaving these flowers... lilacs... into a wreath. Tony, they were the most beautiful lilacs I've ever seen in my whole life. Then she tried it on my head. It was too small." Cassandra paused for a moment. "Tony, we've got to go back tomorrow."

"We can't. We've got to be on that plane. Everyone back home is freaking out."

"She'll be so disappointed," Cassandra said, her eyes starting to fill with tears.

"Who'll be?"

"Cassandra. Little Cassandra. She begged me to come."

"We can't. It's impossible," Tony said.

"But she'll be so disappointed. It's her birthday tomorrow."

"It's *your* birthday, too, you know."

Cassandra gasped. "I completely forgot."

"What else happened back there?"

"I tried to warn her about the battle that was coming and the danger that Troy would be in, but she just laughed. Then her mother was calling her and her brothers... and then I felt myself slipping away. And the whole thing kind of disappeared."

"That was probably when I pried the stone out of your hand."

"The stone?" Cassandra said, thinking back. "Tony! The stone!"

"Don't worry. I have it right here in my pocket."

Cassandra's whole body relaxed. "Oh, Tony." Her eyes filled with tears. Resting her head on Tony's shoulder, she felt herself getting sleepy "It was so beautiful," she murmured. "Do you think it was just a dream? It felt so real." She felt her eyelids getting heavy. "It felt so real."

Tony put his arm around her. Cassandra's eyelids closed as she drifted off to sleep.

Chapter Twenty-One
Café Résat

"We're lucky that we got a table tonight," Tony said, looking around.

"What do you mean?" Cassandra asked. "I see some empty tables."

"The place is going to be packed in a little while. They're having a farewell party for one of the archeologists in charge of the excavations at Troy." Tony paused a moment. "By the way, you look great," he commented. "How do you feel?"

"Much better. The hot shower did wonders."

Just then, there was a commotion at the front of the

restaurant. A group of about twenty people entered. Résat, the owner of the café, walked over to the group to greet them. He turned and said something in Turkish. Waiters and busboys sprang into action, heading for the kitchen, returning with trays of prepared delicacies which they placed on a large buffet table that had been set up in the middle of the room. Café Résat was alive with activity. Turkish music emanated from tiny speakers. Conversation and a sense of excitement filled the air.

"Have you decided?" A waiter standing next to Tony asked.

"I think we need some help," Tony said, staring confusedly at the menu.

At that moment Résat walked by, stopping at their table. The waiter said something to him in Turkish.

"Do you like lamb?" Résat asked, looking at Cassandra.

Cassandra made a face. "Not really," she murmured politely, not wanting to appear rude.

"Then why don't you help yourselves to the buffet. There are many delicious things. You can try a little of each."

"Is it very expensive?" Tony asked.

"No. It's on the house tonight… in honor of Dr. Rose. Only the drinks are extra."

Tony looked at Cassandra. "What do you think?"

"Sounds fine."

"Thank you, Mr. …?" Tony said to Résat, as he and Cassandra got up from their seats.

"Just call me Résat."

Tony nodded.

Tony and Cassandra walked over to the buffet table, which was covered with a wide variety of exotic-looking foods. Other people, including some young women from the archeological team, were already in line. Cassandra was relieved to see that they were wearing slacks. She felt less embarrassed to be wearing her white jeans and a tank top, even though it was her good one… the one decorated with rhinestones. The dress had been just too wet to wear and there hadn't been enough time to go to the laundry room and put it in the dryer.

"Some of these things look like the stuff my dad serves in his restaurant," Cassandra said, using a pair of tongs to lift a couple of stuffed grape leaves onto her plate.

"Then you can help me choose," Tony said.

With Cassandra's guidance, both their plates were soon filled. They headed back to their table and took their seats.

A waiter, approaching their table, asked, "Will you be having wine with your dinner?"

Tony looked up at the waiter. "Do you have Coca Cola?"

"But, of course," the waiter replied. "For both of you?"

Tony looked at Cassandra. She nodded.

"Yes, please," Tony said to the waiter, who was already on his way to the kitchen.

Suddenly there was the sound of applause coming from the other side of the restaurant. About thirty people were on their feet, lifting their glasses in a toast. Only one man remained seated. He was a scholarly-looking gentleman in his mid-forties, with large tortoise-rimmed glasses and medium brown hair that was beginning to gray at the temples. He nodded in modest acknowledgement of their toast.

"Who's that?" Cassandra asked, looking at the seated man.

"That must be Professor Rose," Tony said.

"Professor?" Cassandra asked. "He looks so young."

"Yes," Tony agreed. "He's one of the archeologists in charge of the excavations at Troy. It's called Project Troia."

"That's what's printed on the front of the sweatshirt that the nice lady lent me," Cassandra said.

Tony nodded, then continued. "They have archeologists from all over the world working together as a team."

"How do know all this?" Cassandra asked, taking a bite of one of the stuffed grape leaves on her plate.

"I learned it from the booklet that Maurice was handing out when we got off the bus."

"You read the whole thing?" Cassandra asked, amazed. "It looked huge."

"It just seems like that. It's written in ten different languages. The English part is only about five pages long." Tony took a bite of his food and glanced over at Professor Rose's table. "From what I read, he's one of the leading archeologists in the world."

Cassandra, impressed, looked over at the professor.

"He worked with a very famous German archeologist, who passed away not too long ago. His name was Manfred Korfmann." Tony took a sip of his Coke. "Professor Korfmann's the one who actually started the whole controversy."

"What controversy?" Cassandra asked.

"The one about how big Troy actually was," Tony said.

"What do you mean?" Cassandra put down her fork.

"Do you remember how people didn't even believe that Troy was real, until that German fellow, Schliemann, came along looking for gold?"

"Yes. You told me about it on the bus on the way to Troy."

"Well," Tony continued, "it seems that even after Schliemann had found Troy, people felt that it was only as big as the palace and surrounding walls… since that's all that they had uncovered in their excavations."

Cassandra listened intently, no longer interested in her food. "Go on."

"Dr. Korfmann, believed that Troy had been a much larger city… that it extended way beyond the palace."

"He was right," Cassandra said.

Tony looked at her for a moment, then continued. "Professor Rose worked alongside of Dr. Korfmann for many years. In fact, he was with him when Dr. Korfmann proved his theory."

"What theory?"

"That Troy was much bigger than just the palace… that it was a very large city."

"How did he prove that?" Cassandra asked.

"The area around Troy was too big to dig up and there were no signs that any city had ever been there. So Dr. Korfmann made arrangements for a what's called a geo-magnetic survey… kind of like a taking giant x-ray of the area around the palace."

"And…?"

"The survey showed the underground outline of a huge city."

"That's right!" Cassandra said, starting to get excited.

"How do you know?" Tony asked.

"I saw it," she said. "When I told little Cassandra about the battle that was coming, she took me to the wall and climbed up onto a bench so that she could see. We looked out over the palace wall at the city below." Cassandra paused for a moment. "Tony, it was huge. It was an enormous city. It stretched as far as I could see." She paused again for a moment, then said, "You've got to tell Professor Rose that Dr. Korfmann was right."

Seeing Résat standing at a nearby table talking with some customers, Tony motioned to him. Walking over to Tony, Résat asked, "Is everything alright?"

"Yes. Delicious," Tony said. Clearing his throat, he continued, "Résat, do you think that you could introduce me to Professor Rose?"

"Of course," Résat answered, looking over at the professor, seeing that he was through with his meal. "Come with me."

Tony got up and followed Résat over to Professor Rose's table. Cassandra watched as Résat said something to Dr. Rose. The professor stood up and shook Tony's hand. Cassandra wondered what Tony was saying to him. She saw both Tony and the Professor looking over in her direction. Tony gestured for Cassandra to join them. Getting up from her chair, she walked across the room.

"Dr. Rose, I'd like you to meet Cassandra," Tony said.

"Pleased to meet you, Cassandra," Professor Rose said, extending his right hand.

"Pleased to meet you, too, professor," Cassandra said shyly, shaking his hand.

"Please, call me Brian."

Cassandra smiled.

Professor Rose continued. "Tony said that you had something that you wanted to tell me."

"Yes," Cassandra said. "I wanted to tell you that Dr. Korfmann was right."

"About what?" Professor Rose asked, looking interested.

"About Troy."

"What do you mean?"

"He was right about Troy being a big city."

"How do you know that?" Professor Rose asked.

"I saw it."

Professor Rose remained quiet for a moment. "You *saw* it?"

"Yes. When I looked over the palace wall, I saw many houses."

"How many… ten?… twenty?"

"No. There were hundreds… maybe thousands… as far as I could see."

The professor studied her carefully. "Tell me, Cassandra, have you ever seen any drawings of Troy?"

"No."

Professor Rose thought for moment. "Can you describe what the chimneys on the tops of the houses looked like?"

Cassandra closed her eyes for a moment, remembering back. Opening her eyes, she said, "There were no chimneys. All the roofs were flat."

Professor Rose cleared his throat and turned to Tony. "Has anything like this ever happened to Cassandra before?"

"Sort of," Tony said.

The professor was quiet. After a moment, he reached into the back pocket of his slacks, pulling out two business cards, handing one each to Tony and Cassandra. "How long will you be staying in Çanakkale?"

"We're leaving tomorrow," Tony answered.

The professor thought for a moment. "I'm going to be back in the Philadelphia in a few days. Where do you live?"

"New Jersey," Tony answered.

"I'd like to see Cassandra again. Do you think that the two of you might be able to visit me in Philadelphia sometime after I get back?"

Tony looked at Cassandra. She nodded.

"Sure," Tony said. "It's not that far."

"Great," Professor Rose said. Pulling out another card, along with a ball point pen, handing them to Tony. "Could you write down your phone number in case I need to call you?"

"Of course," Tony said, writing his number on the back of the card. "It's my cell number. You can text me, too, if you like."

"Excellent," the professor said. Glancing briefly at Tony's number, he put the card in his shirt pocket.

Professor Rose, sensing that he was neglecting his colleagues, turned to Cassandra and said, "It's been a pleasure meeting you."

"Same here," Cassandra said.

"And you, too, Tony." He shook Tony's hand and rejoined the people at his table.

Tony and Cassandra walked back to their table and sat down.

Cassandra looked down at the business card that she was holding in her hand. She began reading aloud: "C. Brian Rose. James B. Pritchard Professor of Archaeology, University of Pennsylvania; Curator-in-Charge, Mediterranean Section, Penn Museum of Archaeology and Anthropology." Cassandra looked up at Tony. "It's a good thing I didn't see his card before I met him. I would've been too nervous to talk to him."

"You did fine," Tony said. "I'm very proud of you."

Their waiter appeared. "Would you care for some coffee?"

Tony looked at Cassandra. She shook her head.

"No, thanks," Tony said, looking up at the waiter. "Just the check, please."

Leaving a few liras on the small tray, including a tip for the waiter, Tony and Cassandra stood up to leave. Catching sight of them leaving, Professor Rose waved goodbye. They waved back as they made their way toward the front of the restaurant.

Résat, who was standing by the front door, asked, "Did you enjoy your dinner?"

Tony and Cassandra answered, almost simultaneously,

"Yes, it was delicious."

Tony continued, "And thank you for introducing us to Professor Rose.

"My pleasure," Résat answered, holding the door open for them. "Be sure to come again when you return to Çanakkale."

"We will," Tony said, as he and Cassandra stepped out into the warm night air.

Chapter Twenty-Two

THE VISIT

The tiny red light on the card reader flashed on and off, as Cassandra pushed her room key into the card slot.

"My room key's not working," she said, frustrated.

"Maybe they've already checked us out. They know we're leaving at five a.m.," Tony said. Tony pushed his card key into the slot beside the door to his room. The small green light glowed steadily. "Mine still works." Thinking for a moment, he said, "Did you lock the door between our rooms when we left this morning?"

"No, I don't think so."

"Then come in this way." Turning the handle, Tony

opened the door to his room and switched on the light. He and Cassandra entered the room. "We've got to start packing right away. The wake-up call is coming at four," he said, opening the door to Cassandra's room.

* * *

Tony placed his nearly packed carry-on back on the luggage rack. Walking over to the window, he pulled aside the drapes that covered the sliding door to the balcony. The moon, nearly full and just above the horizon, made the waves seem to glisten. Opening the sliding door, Tony stepped out onto the balcony. The smell of the sea was refreshing after the stale air of the air-conditioned room.

Tony was surprised to see Cassandra standing on her side of the adjoining balcony. She seemed to be in a world of her own, staring at the moon's reflection on the water, her hands resting lightly on the balcony railing. He walked quietly over to her.

"It's almost your birthday," he said, gently.

Cassandra turned to look at him. He noticed that her eyes were filled with tears.

"You're still sad about not being able to go back to Troy tomorrow, aren't you?" Tony asked.

Cassandra nodded. "She's going to be so disappointed."

"We *have* to be on that plane back to the States," Tony said, wiping away a tear from Cassandra's cheek. "I've got a whole bunch of text messages from Uncle Dan, telling me that he's been trying his best to keep everyone at bay. He says that he can't hold them off much longer." Tony paused, wiping away another tear. "He and Mikéli are the only ones who know that we're here. Everyone else thinks we're in Athens."

"I know," Cassandra said. "I just can't stop thinking about how disappointed she'll be." Cassandra looked at Tony. "You were going to be there, too, you know."

"What do you mean?" Tony asked.

"When I was sitting at the table where little Cassandra was weaving that beautiful wreath of lilacs, she told me that Helenus, her twin brother, had invited Anthony, his best friend... and that *she* could invite someone, too. She wanted *me* to come." Cassandra couldn't hold back the tears any longer. They streamed down her cheeks.

Tony pulled her close and hugged her. "She'll understand."

"How do you know?" Cassandra asked, through her tears.

"I just know," Tony said. He held her for a moment, saying nothing.

Tony could feel that her crying was subsiding. He glanced at his watch. *Two minutes past midnight.* He wanted to tell her that it was her birthday, but somehow knew that it was not the right time.

"What if it didn't really happen?" Cassandra murmured.

"What?" Tony asked, pulling away slightly.

Cassandra looked directly into his eyes. "What if I imagined the whole thing?"

Tony looked at her. "We'll never know." He paused. "By the way... Happy Birthday," Tony said, kissing her gently on the cheek.

Cassandra, still as if in another world, murmured, "It felt so real."

"So will the wake-up call when it comes in less than four hours," Tony said.

Cassandra tried to smile. "I'm not sleepy."

"You will be," Tony said. "Are you packed?"

"No."

"You'd better get started. You'll be too tired when we wake up."

"Tony?"

"What?"

"Can we sleep with the door between our rooms open tonight?"

Tony thought for a moment, trying to be responsible. "Sure."

*　　*　　*

Cassandra touched her white dress that she had hung on the back of the bathroom door. *It's still too damp. I'll pack it when I wake up.* Putting on her nightgown, she walked over to the bed, threw back the covers and climbed in. She lay there for a few minutes, then called out, "Tony?"

"What?"

"I'm not sleepy."

"You better be. The wake-up call is coming in three hours."

"G'nite," Cassandra said.

"G'nite," Tony answered.

In spite of herself, Cassandra began to feel drowsy. Turning out the lamp on the nightstand, she pulled the covers up and soon felt herself drifting off to sleep.

*　　*　　*

"Wake up. Wake up," a voice said.

Cassandra felt someone tugging at her arm.

"Wake up. Wake up."

"Tony?" Cassandra said, half asleep.

"Wake up. We don't have much time."

Cassandra slowly opened her eyes. There before her stood little Cassandra, dressed in a white dress similar to the one the day before, but more festive. Her hair was pulled up in a decorative style.

Suddenly Cassandra became alert. She sat up in bed.

"I knew you couldn't come today," little Cassandra said. "I have something for you." She held out before her a wreath of white lilacs.

Cassandra got out of bed.

"Try it on," little Cassandra said. "Try it on. I made it just for you."

Cassandra bent down.

Little Cassandra placed the wreath on Cassandra's head and smiled joyfully. "It fits! It fits," she said. "I knew it would."

Standing up, Cassandra reached up with both her hands and gently touched the beautiful lilac crown.

"I can't stay long," little Cassandra said. "I had to sneak away."

Cassandra eyes began to fill with tears.

"Don't cry," little Cassandra said. "We'll see each other again. I promise." Little Cassandra stood on tiptoe and kissed Cassandra on the cheek.

Suddenly the sound of the telephone ringing shattered

the silence. Little Cassandra was gone.

Cassandra rolled over in bed and answered the phone on her nightstand. The line was dead. She looked at the clock. *4:00 a.m.* It was the wakeup call. Quickly getting out of bed, still dressed in her nightgown, she ran into Tony's room. Tony was fumbling with the phone.

"Tony. Tony. Wake up. Wake up. I just had the most incredible dream."

Tony, half asleep, sat up in bed. Cassandra sat down next to him.

"What about?" he asked.

"Little Cassandra… I dreamt about her."

Tony looked at Cassandra, questioningly.

"She came to me. She brought the wreath that she said she was going to make for me. She wanted to see if it would fit. She knew that I couldn't come for her birthday. You were right, Tony. You were right."

Tony looked at her, groggily.

"She said that she didn't have much time. She promised that we'd see each other again and kissed me on the cheek. Then the phone rang and she vanished." Cassandra paused briefly. "Tony, it was such a beautiful dream. She looked so lovely… with her white dress and her hair all fixed up. Oh, Tony… it seemed so real."

Standing up, Tony gently rested his hand on Cassandra's shoulder. "You'll have to tell me about your dream later. We've got to get ready. The cab'll be here in half an hour. Don't forget, we have to drop that sweatshirt off at the front desk."

"I know," Cassandra said. Getting up, she headed back

to her room.

"Tony!" she screamed from the doorway. "C'mere! Quick!"

Alarmed, Tony ran over to where she was standing.

Cassandra pointed to the foot of the bed.

There, amongst the covers, lay the lilac wreath. It appeared to be glowing in the dimly lit room.

Tony and Cassandra stood staring at it.

"She was *here*!" Cassandra said. "It *wasn't* a dream!"

~ Cassandra ~

Chapter Twenty-Three

FLIGHT SEVENTY-THREE

"Ladies and Gentlemen, welcome John F. Kennedy International Airport," the flight attendant announced. "Local time is 4:36 PM. We ask that you remain in your seats until the airplane has come to a complete halt. We hope that you've enjoyed flying Delta and look forward to seeing you again soon."

The sound of seat belts being undone filled the cabin. Tony and Cassandra stood up. Reaching up and unlatching the luggage compartment, Tony pulled out both his and Cassandra's carry-on bags and set them down on the floor of the cabin.

"Do you think the wreath's all right?" Cassandra asked.

"Did you pack it like I told you?" Tony responded.

"Yes, I put it between my t-shirt and my dress. I hope it didn't get crushed."

"That's the least of my worries," Tony said.

"What do you mean?"

"We still have to go through Customs. They don't allow plants to be brought in from another country. If they find it, they'll confiscate it."

"Oh, no!" Cassandra said, alarmed. "What'll we do?"

"Let's just hope they don't open your suitcase," Tony answered.

* * *

On the other side of the glass partition marked "U.S. Customs", Dana and Maria waved excitedly. Cassandra could see Maria dab at her eyes with a tissue. Tony and Cassandra waved back at their mothers as they inched forward in the line leading up to the customs inspection counter.

Soon Cassandra was at the front of the line. A uniformed Customs officer gestured for her to step forward. She approached the counter, pulling her carry-on behind her.

The inspector smiled, then asked, "Do you have anything to declare?"

Cassandra froze. "What do you mean?"

"Are you bringing anything into the country that you didn't have with you when you left?" he asked.

The color drained from Cassandra's face. "I... I've never done this before," she said, nervously.

"That's okay, miss. Just put your suitcase up here on the counter and open it for me."

She glanced back at Tony, who nodded for her to comply.

Cassandra held her breath as she placed her suitcase on the counter and opened it. A light sweat broke out on her forehead. She felt as if she were about to faint. The inspector began to rifle through her clothes. Cassandra's heart began to pound as the customs inspector lifted the white dress up out of the suitcase, revealing the t-shirt upon which she had placed the wreath.

It's not there! The wreath was gone. Cassandra looked at Tony and mouthed the words, "It's not there."

Tony, who was standing close enough to have observed the whole procedure, shrugged his shoulders in bewilderment.

"You can put your things back now, miss," the inspector said, his voice snapping Cassandra back to reality. He wrote something on his clipboard, then gestured for Tony to approach the counter.

* * *

"Your father had a cake sent over from the restaurant," Maria said, as she turned the key in the front door.

Cassandra grimaced. "Is the custody hearing still on?"

"Yes, it's scheduled for Tuesday," Maria answered.

Cassandra and Tony looked at each other.

"Can you stay for a piece of cake?" Maria asked Dana, as they entered the house.

"Of course, but just for a few minutes. Bill will be home soon and will be wanting to see Tony."

"I want to take my suitcase upstairs," Cassandra said.

"Let me help you," Tony said, picking up her carry-on and heading up the stairs. Cassandra followed closely behind.

"Come back down soon," Maria called after them.

"We will," Cassandra said, following Tony up the stairs and into her room.

"Where do you want me to put it?" Tony asked.

"On my bed, thanks."

Tony placed Cassandra's suitcase on the bed. "I'll meet you downstairs," he said. Turning, he started to leave the room.

Cassandra unzipped the suitcase and flipped the top open.

"Tony!" she screamed.

Already halfway down the stairs, Tony turned and ran back up to Cassandra's room.

"What is it?" Tony asked, entering the room.

"Look!" Cassandra said, pointing at the opened suitcase. There, on top of the dress, in perfection condition, lay the beautiful wreath of white lilacs.

"How did she do it?" Cassandra asked.

"I don't know," Tony said, staring at the wreath.

"Cassandra! Tony!" Maria called from the kitchen. "Dana has to leave soon. Tony's father will be wanting to see him."

"Tony, can you go downstairs and keep them busy for a minute?" Cassandra asked.

"Sure," he said, sensing that she needed to be alone. Tony turned and headed for the stairs.

Holding her breath, Cassandra walked slowly over to her bed, gently lifting the lilac wreath from the suitcase. "How did you *do* it?" she asked half-aloud.

Suddenly, the room was filled with the faint echo of a child's mischievous laughter. Cassandra recognized the laugh as that of little Cassandra.

Walking over to the bureau, Cassandra carefully placed the wreath on her head and looked at herself in the mirror. "It fits perfectly," she said, half aloud.

As if from far away, Cassandra heard the voice of little Cassandra. "I told you… I made it just for you."

"Cassandra!" Maria called from downstairs.

"I have to go," Cassandra whispered, carefully removing the lilac wreath and placing it gently on her bureau.

Once again, the sound of a child's laughter echoed throughout the room.

"I love it," Cassandra said softly, "… and I love you, too."

~ Cassandra ~

Chapter Twenty-Four

THE CONFRONTATION

"Does your mother know that you're going to meet with your father?" Tony asked, pulling into the parking lot of Nikos' restaurant.

"No, I didn't tell her," Cassandra answered.

"Are you sure you want to go through with this?"

"Yes," Cassandra said, a determined look on her face. "I called him earlier this morning."

"What'd you tell him?"

"I told him that I had to talk with him about something."

"And what did he say?"

"He told me to be here around noon."

Tony looked at the clock on the dashboard of the car, which read 11:54. "How long do you think you're going to be?"

"It shouldn't take more than half an hour."

"I'll wait right here," Tony said, reassuringly.

"Thanks," she said.

Bracing herself for what she knew would be an unpleasant encounter, Cassandra got out of the car and walked across the parking lot to the front entrance of the Olympia Restaurant.

Tony watched as she opened the door and walked inside.

* * *

Tony looked down at the clock on the dashboard... *12:05.*

The lunchtime crowd had begun to arrive at the restaurant. Several customers, milling around the entrance, blocked his view of the front door.

Starting to get anxious, Tony checked the clock again... *12:15.*

At that moment, Tony saw Cassandra come out of the restaurant. She walked quickly over to his car, opened the passenger door and got in.

"That was fast," Tony said. "How'd it go?"

"Not well," Cassandra replied, a grim look on her face.

"What'd he say?" Tony asked, starting the engine and slowly pulling out of the parking lot.

"He said that Petros is a crazy old fool... and that everything he told us is nonsense."

"Do you think he knows that Petros died?"

"He didn't act like he knew," Cassandra said, "but I couldn't tell for sure."

"Did you mention the list?"

"No."

Tony and Cassandra were quiet for a while, as Tony drove home.

"So what are you going to do now?" he asked, breaking the silence.

"I don't know," Cassandra answered.

*   *   *

As Tony made the turn onto Oak Street, Cassandra felt her cell phone vibrate. Looking down at the caller I.D., she answered, "Hi, Mom. What's up?"

"Where are you?" Maria asked.

"We're on our way there," Cassandra said. "We're just up the street."

"Okay, bye," Maria said, hanging up the phone.

As Tony and Cassandra approached the house, they saw Maria running down the front path waiving her arms, directing Tony to pull the car into the driveway. Tony turned into the driveway and stopped the engine. Cassandra opened the car door and stepped out.

"What is it, Mom?" Cassandra asked.

"Your father just called. He's dropping the custody case," Maria said, tears of happiness running down her face.

Cassandra hugged her mother.

"My baby can stay with me," Maria said, through her tears. "My baby can stay with me."

Cassandra looked over Maria's shoulder at Tony, who had gotten out of the car and was standing a few feet away.

"I'll call you later," Tony said. "You two need some time together."

Cassandra nodded.

Tony got back in the car and started the engine. He watched as Cassandra and Maria walked back into the house.

Chapter Twenty-Five
PROFESSOR ROSE

Cassandra awoke slowly, forgetting for a moment where she was. Upon opening her eyes, she was startled to see Maria sitting on the edge of her bed, crying.

"Mom, what's the matter?" Cassandra asked, alarmed.

"Nothing's the matter," Maria replied. "I'm just so happy that you're home."

"Oh, Mom," Cassandra said, sitting up and hugging her mother. "Don't cry."

Reaching over to her nightstand, Cassandra pulled a tissue from the box.

"Please don't cry," she said, dabbing at her mother's tears.

"I'll be alright," Maria said, getting up from the bed. "Would you like me to make you some breakfast?"

"No, it's okay. I'm not really hungry." Cassandra glanced at the clock radio on her nightstand. *8:37.* "Maybe a glass of orange juice," she said, getting out of bed.

Just then, Cassandra heard the familiar sound of Tony's ring tone on her cell phone.

"Hey, Tony. What's up?" Cassandra asked, speaking into the phone.

"Can you talk?"

"Sure."

"Professor Rose just called," Tony said. "He'd like to see us today."

"Today?" Cassandra asked.

"Yes. Can you make it? It's only about a forty minute drive."

"I don't know. I have to ask Mom. I'll call you right back." Cassandra ended the call. Turning to Maria, she said, "Mom? Tony wants to know if I can go with him today to see Professor Rose."

"Who's Professor Rose?"

Cassandra walked over to her desk, opened the drawer and retrieved the professor's card. Handing it to Maria, she said, "He's an archeologist that Tony and I met when we were in Troy."

"Troy?" Maria asked, surprised. "That's in Turkey. You didn't tell me you were going to Troy. What were you doing there?"

"It's a long story, Mom. I'll tell you later."

Looking at the card, Maria said, "Why does he want to see you?"

"I think he wants to ask us some questions about our visit to Troy."

"But he's in Philadelphia."

"It's not that far. Tony said it would only take about forty minutes to get there."

"You just got home and you're leaving again?"

"Please, Mom. It'll only be for a few hours."

Maria thought for a moment. "Will you be home in time for dinner?"

"I'm pretty sure."

"Okay," Maria sighed, realizing that there was no point in trying to change Cassandra's mind.

Cassandra swiped the screen on her cell phone. She touched Tony's contact number and held the phone to her ear.

"What's happening?" Tony asked.

"Mom said it's okay. What time should I be ready?"

"I'll be there in half an hour."

* * *

Tony turned the car into the parking lot of the Penn Museum. "The campus looks huge," he remarked.

Cassandra nodded, taking in the surroundings.

Pulling into a parking space, Tony turned off the engine. He and Cassandra got out of the car and headed for the main entrance to the museum. They walked through the impressive-looking opened doors. On the side wall of the entrance foyer was a directory. Quickly scanning the list of departments, Tony said, "There it is.

Mediterranean Section – Office of the Curator." Tony looked around. "Let's take the stairs." Tony and Cassandra headed for the nearby stairwell.

*　　*　　*

On the heavy oak door of the office was a brass plaque, which read: Dr. C. Brian Rose. Curator-In-Charge. Tony knocked on the partially opened door.

"Come in," a man's voice called out from inside the office.

Tony slowly opened the door and entered, followed by Cassandra. Built-in bookcases filled with books covered the walls. Drawings and photographs of archeological expeditions occupied whatever space was left on the walls. In front of a large window was an old mahogany desk covered with stacks of papers, behind which sat Professor Rose.

"Tony! Cassandra! Thanks for making the trip. It's great to see you again," Professor Rose said, getting up from his chair. He walked around the desk to greet Tony and Cassandra.

"Professor Rose," Tony said, extending his right hand.

"Call me Brian," he said, shaking Tony's hand, then extending his hand to Cassandra.

Smiling shyly, Cassandra shook Brian's hand.

"I'm so glad that you could come," he said, warmly. "Have a seat." He pointed to two guest chairs in front of his desk. "There's some bottled water in the fridge. Would you care for some?"

"No, thank you," Tony and Cassandra said, almost in unison. They took their seats.

Brian walked around his desk and sat down. Turning to Cassandra, he said, "I have so many questions to ask you."

Cassandra sat up straight in her chair, feeling a little nervous.

"As you know, I've been working at the Troy site for many years now. We've uncovered a great deal of information about the past, much of which has been scientifically verified."

Tony and Cassandra listened attentively.

"But this is the first time," Brian continued, "that there might be an opportunity to have visual confirmation of what things actually looked like in Troy." He looked directly at Cassandra. "When I first met you at Café Résat, you told that you had 'seen' Troy."

Cassandra nodded.

"For years now, there's been one question on my mind to which I've been trying to find the answer," Brian said.

"What's that?" Cassandra asked.

"What were the women doing during the attack?"

Cassandra looked at the professor, confused by the question. "What attack?"

"The attack on Troy… by the Greek army."

"There was no attack when I was there," Cassandra said. "Everything was peaceful and beautiful."

"Do you have any idea what year it was when you were there?"

"I have no idea. All I know is that Cassandra was eight years old. It was the day before her ninth birthday."

"You actually saw Cassandra?"

"Yes… and her brothers, too. Helenus, Hector and Paris. I even saw her mother standing on the palace steps."

"You *saw* Hecuba?"

"I didn't know her name… Cassandra called her 'mother' when she spoke to her."

Brian sat back in his chair, thinking for a moment. "If Cassandra was eight," he mused aloud, "then what you saw probably occurred about ten years before the attack on Troy." He paused a moment, then continued. "I have some drawings I'd like to show you, Cassandra." Opening his desk drawer, he retrieved two large manila folders and placed them on top of his desk. "These are some artist's renderings of what Troy was supposed to have looked like during the different periods of its existence," Brian said, opening one of the folders.

Tony leaned forward in his chair to get a better look.

"Did you know that there were nine different cities, all named Troy?" Brian asked Tony.

"Maurice told our tour group about it on the bus, but he was speaking in French so I missed a lot of what he was saying."

Brian nodded, then continued. "Each new city was built on top of the remains of the previous city." Turning to Cassandra, he asked, "Do you remember what you saw in Troy?"

"Yes. It was beautiful," Cassandra said.

Holding up a drawing of a palace that looked like the Parthenon in Greece, Brian asked, "Did it look like this?"

"No, not at all," Cassandra answered.

Brian looked at her. "What about this?" he asked, holding up another drawing.

"No," she replied.

"Okay." Brian held up yet another drawing. "How about this one?"

"No," Cassandra said, a note of disappointment in her voice.

Brian sighed deeply, closed the folder and leaned back in his chair. He studied Cassandra for a moment.

A light sweat broke out on Cassandra's forehead. She began to feel tears stinging at her eyes. *He doesn't believe me. He probably thinks I'm crazy*, Cassandra thought to herself.

"In Café Résat," Brian said, "you told me that Troy was a large city."

Cassandra nodded, feeling that she had disappointed him.

"Where were you when you saw the city?"

"On the terrace with Cassandra."

"The terrace?"

"Yes… the terrace in front of the palace. We were standing by the palace wall when I saw the city," Cassandra said.

"But the palace wall was too high for you to see over."

Cassandra's started to cry. "I'm sorry, Professor… I mean Brian. I feel like I'm disappointing you, but none of the drawings that you've shown me look anything like what I saw in Troy… and I *did* see over the palace wall."

Seeing her tears, Brian realized that he had gone too far in his attempt to test Cassandra's credibility. Opening the other manila folder, he said, "I have one more drawing that I'd like you to see."

Cassandra nodded, wiping away some tears with the back of her hand.

"What do think of this one?" Brian asked, trying to act nonchalant.

"That's it! That's it!" she said, excitedly, getting to her feet.

Brian felt the hairs on his arms stand up. *This girl's the real thing*, he thought to himself. The teenager sitting in front of him had properly identified the Troy of the Trojan War, which Homer had described in the Iliad… the Troy of King Priam, and his wife, Hecuba… and their children, Hector, Paris, Helenus… and the doomed prophetess, Cassandra.

Cassandra looked closely at the drawing. "This is it. This is it. But some things aren't correct."

Brian leaned forward in his chair, listening intently to her every word. "Like what?"

"The palace wall is too high. The terrace was made of smooth marble tiles. The tables didn't look like that at all. And the steps to the palace were in a different place."

Taking a pencil from a cup on his desk, Brian handed it to Cassandra. "Go ahead… you can sketch what you saw on this drawing. It's just a copy," he said, turning the drawing so that it faced Cassandra.

"I can't draw very well," she said, apologetically.

"It doesn't matter. Just do the best that you can," Brian said. He watched, fascinated, as Cassandra stood at his desk making changes to the drawing… first lowering the wall… then changing the tables from square to round.

"The palace steps were over *here*", Cassandra said, pointing to a different place than the steps were pictured in the drawing.

Brian watched as Cassandra made changes to the drawing. She was drawing quickly now, her strokes more confident. Her face was flushed with excitement. When she stopped, he turned the drawing toward him so that he could better view it.

"Fabulous!" he said, studying the drawing intensely. "You've done well, Cassandra."

Cassandra smiled, her tears gone.

"Cassandra, I owe you an apology," Brian said, clearing his throat. "Before… when I showed you the first few drawings, I was just testing you. I knew that they weren't your Troy. I just wanted to find out if you were for real." Brian cleared his throat again, surprised at his own emotionality. "I had no idea that it would upset you so much."

"I felt that I had disappointed you," Cassandra said.

"You haven't disappointed me at all," Brian said. "I never should have doubted you."

~ Cassandra ~

Chapter Twenty-Six

THE TAVERN BY THE SEA

"Oh, Mom. It's beautiful!" Cassandra said, holding up the new white lace-trimmed summer dress in front of her. "You shouldn't have."

"I washed your other white dress," Maria said. "When I hung it up to dry, it really looked ragged. What happened to it?"

"We got caught in a rainstorm," Cassandra said.

"It seems to have shrunk two sizes. So while you and Tony were in Philadelphia, I ran over to the mall."

Cassandra held the dress up to her shoulders. "It's just perfect," she said. "I'll wear it tonight for Tony."

"What's happening tonight?" Maria asked.

"Tony's taking me out for dinner at The Tavern. He says that we didn't get a chance to celebrate my birthday while we were traveling."

"I love that place," Maria said. "You father and I used to go there often."

"Do you miss him, Mom?" Cassandra asked, noticing a look of sadness come over her mother's face.

"A little."

"Do you think you'll get back together?"

Before Maria could answer, Tony's ring tone sounded on Cassandra's cell phone.

"Hey, Tony," Cassandra answered. "What's up?"

"I'm in the Bio-Medical Department at Rutgers."

"What are you doing *there?*"

"They say that they can preserve the wreath by doing something called 'vacuum freezing'."

"What's that?" Cassandra asked.

"I'll explain it to you tonight," Tony said. "They say we got it to them just in time. It would have died in just a few more days."

"When can I have it back?"

"Hopefully, in about a week."

"A week!!!"

"Listen, that's quick. Other places take two to three weeks… and charge up to nine hundred dollars."

"Oh my gosh! How much will this cost?"

"Nothing. They're doing it as a favor to my dad."

"That's fabulous!"

"One more thing. A couple of sprigs and petals fell off

the wreath."

"Oh, no!"

"Don't worry," Tony said, reassuringly. "I have them in a safe place. I also called Brian a little while ago. He and the head of the lab discussed how to handle the wreath. Look, I've got to go. I'll pick you up at seven. Is that okay?"

"See you at seven," Cassandra said, ending the call.

*　*　*

"I wanted to take you to a nice restaurant for dinner," Tony said, turning his car into the parking lot of The Tavern, "but I really can't afford it these days."

"Don't be silly. This is perfect," Cassandra replied. "Besides, I hear they have the best cheeseburgers in the world."

Tony pulled into a parking space directly under a pole lamp. The bright light from the lamp above glinted across the windshield revealing a long crack.

"What happened to your windshield?" Cassandra asked. "I didn't even notice it until now."

"I was on my way back from Rutgers when this rock just flew up from the road and hit the windshield," Tony said. "It was kind of weird because there were no other cars or trucks around."

"That's awful," Cassandra said.

"Don't worry about it," Tony replied. "It just means that it's going to take a little longer for me to pay Uncle Dan back for the flight and the hotel."

"I've got to help, too," Cassandra said.

Tony and Cassandra got out of the car. The warm

breeze coming off the ocean was fresh and invigorating.

"Mmmm! Smells great," Cassandra said, taking a deep breath of the ocean air.

Walking around to where she was standing, Tony said, "You look beautiful. I never saw you in that dress before."

"Mom got it for me yesterday."

"Anyway, you look great."

Cassandra smiled. "You don't look so bad yourself," she said, taking note of how handsome Tony looked in his sports jacket and tie."

Once a privately owned beach house, The Tavern had been converted to a restaurant, which was now well known for its friendly atmosphere, good food and afford-able prices. Perched on the roof, was an old two-sided il-luminated sign that could be seen both from the highway and the beach.

Tony and Cassandra climbed the well-worn wooden steps to the entrance of The Tavern. As Tony opened the door, the sound of an old Wurlitzer jukebox pumping out popular songs filled the air.

"It's really packed," Cassandra said.

"I'm glad I made a reservation. I almost didn't," Tony said. He and Cassandra walked toward a man who stood behind a captain's desk, taking down the names of people who were trying to get a table.

The mood was casual, the crowd young. Most of the men were wearing jackets. The bar was crowded with sin-gles and young couples enjoying themselves.

"Name?" The manager asked Tony in a friendly, but business-like manner.

"Petrarkos," Tony replied.

"Here you are," he said, crossing off Tony's name, then gesturing for a waitress. The waitress led Tony and Cassandra to a red vinyl booth. She placed two menus on the table as Tony and Cassandra slid into their seats.

"I'll be right back," the waitress said. "Would you like something to drink?"

"Two cokes, please," Tony said.

Scribbling the order down on a pad, the waitress hurried off.

Cassandra took a moment to look out the large picture window at the rustic wooden deck, beyond which lay the beach and the ocean. White, Japanese-style paper lanterns that had been hung around the deck, swayed gently in the breeze.

The waitress reappeared with two large, frosted mugs filled to the brim with Coca Cola and crushed ice. She produced a small chalkboard, on which were scrawled the specials of the day.

"No need for that," Tony said. "We know what we want. Two Tavern cheeseburgers with fries."

Jotting down the order, the waitress quickly headed for the kitchen, skillfully maneuvering around some people that were dancing on the small dance floor near the jukebox.

Just then, Cassandra's cell phone chimed and buzzed. Looking down at her phone, she said, "Oh, good."

"What's up?" Tony asked.

"Your mom and mine are going to the movies. She said they'll be home around eleven."

"Great. My dad's been out of town on a lecture tour for the past week."

"I'm glad your mother's taking Mom to the movies," Cassandra said.

Sensing a sadness come over Cassandra, Tony asked, "What's going on with your folks?"

"I don't know. I asked Mom if she missed my father and she said 'kind of'."

"Did you tell her anything about…?"

"No. I didn't say a word. I think it's better if she doesn't know… at least for now." Taking a straw from the holder resting on the table, she removed the thin paper wrapper and pushed the straw down through the crushed ice in her Coke. She took a sip, then looked up at Tony. "Tell me about the wreath," she said.

"They're going to try to preserve it."

"How?"

"It's called vacuum freezing."

"You said that on the phone, but you also said that you'd explain it to me."

"They freeze the wreath and remove the moisture from it while it's frozen. Then, once all the moisture has been extracted, they slowly thaw it out. It'll be just like new."

"Amazing," Cassandra said.

"It'll still be very fragile," Tony added. "You'll have to keep it inside of a glass frame or box, but you'll be able to keep it for a long time to come."

The waitress appeared with two large cheeseburger platters, placing one each in front of Tony and Cassandra.

*   *   *

Music played on the outdoor speakers that had been mounted on the exterior of The Tavern. Tony and Cassandra stood side by side on the wooden deck, leaning against the wood railing as they looked out to sea.

"That was delicious," Cassandra said.

One of Cassandra's favorite songs started playing on the jukebox. She looked at Tony. He turned to face her. Without saying a word, he put his arms around her waist. Cassandra put her arms around Tony's neck. They moved slowly to the music.

After a few moments, Tony pulled back.

"What's the matter?" Cassandra asked.

"I have something for you," Tony said. Reaching into his pocket, he pulled out a small gift-wrapped box. "I never did give you a birthday gift."

"Oh, Tony. You shouldn't have."

"Go ahead," Tony said. "Open it."

Cassandra carefully tore open the wrapping, revealing a jewelry box marked, 'Crestview Jewelers'. She lifted the top of the box. Inside was a small gold heart outline resting on a delicate gold chain.

"Oh, Tony," Cassandra said. "It's beautiful."

"Put it on," he said.

Cassandra lifted the heart and chain out of the box. Handing the box to Tony, Cassandra put the necklace around her neck and tried to connect the clasp.

Seeing that she was having trouble, Tony said, "Let me help."

Cassandra pulled her long brown hair to one side so

that Tony could connect the clasp. She let her hair fall back down.

"I have something else for you," Tony said.

"Something else?"

"Yes," Tony said, pulling out another small jewelry box and handing it to Cassandra.

Lifting the top off the box, she saw a small clear glass-like pendant. There was something inside of it. It looked like a flower petal. Cassandra looked closely at it for a moment. Then it hit her. It was a petal from the lilac wreath that little Cassandra had given to her.

"Oh, Tony!" Cassandra was speechless for a moment. Tears welled up in her eyes. "How did you *do* this?"

"There's a place downtown that does this kind of stuff."

Undoing the clasp of the necklace, Cassandra added the pendant so that it hung next to the gold heart. Putting the necklace back on, she closed the clasp.

"Now I have something from two of the people most precious to me next to my heart. I will wear them forever." The tears that had been forming in her eyes now spilled over onto her cheeks.

Taking a handkerchief from his jacket pocket, Tony started to dry her tears. Cassandra looked up at him.

"Tony…," she started to say.

"I love you," he said, gently touching his lips to hers.

They kissed, holding each other close for a long moment. The strains of a pop love song drifted out onto the deck. Still holding onto each other, they moved as one to the music. Out of the corner of her eye, Cassandra noticed a lone seagull perched on the railing of the deck. It seemed to be watching their every move.

Tony felt Cassandra's body stiffen.

"What's the matter?" he asked, pulling slightly away.

"There's a seagull over there," Cassandra said. "I think he's looking at us."

Tony looked over his shoulder at the bird. "He probably just wants some food."

"No, Tony. He's really staring at us."

Suddenly, without any provocation, the seagull flew off its perch and headed straight for Cassandra. It started pecking at her hair and neck.

"Tony!" she screamed. "Make it stop!"

Tony punched at the seagull, trying his best to hit it, but the bird deftly avoided each of Tony's blows and continued its attack on Cassandra.

"Let's get out of here!" Tony said. Grabbing Cassandra by the hand, he pulled her toward the doorway of The Tavern.

At that moment, the huge sign that had been on the roof of The Tavern came crashing down onto the deck, landing right where Tony and Cassandra had been standing only seconds before. Light bulbs exploded. Glass from the sign splintered, flying everywhere. A large piece of jagged metal was stuck in the wood of the deck.

"Oh, my God!" Cassandra said.

Tony looked pale. He held tightly to Cassandra's hand.

"That seagull saved us," Cassandra said. "He was trying to warn us. He was trying to get us to move out of the way. It's like he *knew* that it was going to happen."

People from inside The Tavern, who had heard the

sound of the sign crashing onto the deck, were now starting to crowd into the open doorway, trying to get a better look.

The manager rushed over to Tony and Cassandra. "Are you two all right?" he asked. "I saw you standing right where the sign fell."

"Yes, we're okay," Tony said, surprised at the shakiness in his voice. Still holding Cassandra by the hand, Tony looked around for the seagull.

It was nowhere to be seen.

Chapter Twenty-Seven

CLOSE CALL

A loud crack of thunder awoke Cassandra from her sleep. The sky was dark. Cassandra could hear the sound of rain pelting against her window. She glanced over at the clock radio on her nightstand. *9:35*. The phone in the kitchen rang twice. Cassandra heard her mother answer.

Moments later, Maria appeared in the bedroom doorway.

"Honey, that was Tony," Maria said. "He's been trying to call you."

Cassandra looked over at the desk, where her cell phone was charging in its cradle.

"He says your phone is turned off." Maria continued. "He's has to leave to do some errands. He said he'll be stopping by in about ten minutes to drop something off."

Cassandra slowly got out of bed and slipped into a pair of jeans.

* * *

Opening the front door to see Tony standing on the porch, wet from having run through the rain from his car, Cassandra said, "Hey, Tony. Come on in."

"I can't stay long," he said, stepping inside. "I've got something for you." Reaching into his pants pocket, Tony pulled out a small fabric pouch with a drawstring. Seeing the quizzical look on Cassandra's face, he said, "It's the stone."

"The stone? Oh, my gosh. Thank you."

"I have one more that I had put in my pocket. I got it for Katrina. When I mentioned it to her this morning, she said that she was anxious to see it. I told her I'd drop it off today."

"But the weather is awful," Cassandra protested. "Do you have to drive into the city today?"

"Don't worry. I'll be alright."

Cassandra looked concerned.

"By the way," Tony continued, "Brian called and asked me about one of the sprigs that had fallen off of the wreath. He and the head of the lab at Rutgers want to send it to the University of Arizona in Tucson, where they do radiocarbon dating."

"What's that?"

"It's a way of telling how old something is."

"I know how old it is."

"I know you do. But it's important to Brian," Tony said. "The sprig that they have has a little bit of thread on it and they want to test it out."

"What do you think I should do?"

"I think you should let them send it. I just wanted to check with you first."

Cassandra thought for a moment, then said, "I guess it's okay."

Reaching into his shirt pocket, Tony pulled out a small box. "Here... I have something else for you."

"Another gift?"

"Not really," Tony said, handing the small box to Cassandra.

Cassandra lifted the lid off the box, revealing the other sprig that had fallen off the lilac wreath.

"Oh, Tony!" Cassandra said, moved at seeing a piece of the wreath again.

"It's already starting to wilt," Tony said, "but I knew that you'd want it anyway."

Cassandra nodded. "Thank you."

"Look. I've got to run," Tony said, giving Cassandra a quick kiss on the cheek. "See you later."

"See you," Cassandra said. "Say hi to Katrina for me."

Tony turned and ran out into the rain toward his car.

* * *

Sitting at her desk, Cassandra loosened the drawstring on the pouch containing the stone. She emptied the stone into the palm of her right hand and closed her eyes. She waited. Nothing happened. She concentrated harder.

Again nothing.

Opening her eyes, Cassandra put the stone back in the pouch and drew the string taut.

Getting up from her desk, she walked over to her bureau. Opening the top drawer, she put the pouch containing the stone and the box with the sprig in the drawer and gently closed the drawer. Glancing at herself in the mirror, she noticed the beautiful heart and pendant that Tony had given her the night before. Reaching up, she held the gold heart in her hand.

Suddenly, Cassandra's body stiffened. Her fists clenched. Her eyes were opened wide, unblinking. What she saw was no longer her reflection in the mirror, but instead the view from behind a steering wheel. Rain poured down from the sky splashing onto the windshield. The wipers swept back and forth. The sky was dark. Looking up at the rearview mirror, she saw two bright headlights bearing down on her from behind.

"Tony!" she screamed, as she came out of her trance. Quickly grabbing her cell phone from its cradle, she placed a call to Tony.

"Hi, this is Tony," the voice-mail announced. "I can't take your call right now. Please leave a message and I'll call you right back."

"Oh, my God," Cassandra said out loud.

She quickly dialed Katrina's cell number.

"Hello?" Katrina answered.

"Katrina, it's me… Cassandra. Did Tony get there yet?"

"He left about fifteen minutes ago."

"Oh, no!" Cassandra moaned.

"What's the matter?" Katrina asked.

"He's going to have an accident. I saw it." She paused for a moment. "I've got to go. Speak to you later." Cassandra ended the call.

*   *   *

Traffic on the George Washington Bridge was heavy. The relentless rain had brought the traffic to a near stand-still. Tony pulled up to the booth, handing the toll taker the correct change. Driving into the plaza on the New Jersey side of the bridge, Tony followed the signs for the Garden State Parkway. Thinking that he might avoid some traffic, he pulled off onto Highway 17. He was right. Traffic was flowing smoothly, hardly a car on the road. Tony was pleased with his choice of routes.

Glancing up at the rearview mirror, Tony noticed a large black SUV with tinted windows and bright lights on, following a little too closely behind him. He looked at the speedometer. *55 miles per hour.* Concerned about the hazardous driving conditions, Tony reluctantly accelerated, in an effort put some distance between the two vehicles. *61 miles per hour.* He glanced again at the mirror. The SUV was now even closer than before. Tony could see that the SUV was only about ten feet behind and bearing down on him. He stepped on the gas. *67 miles per hour.* The SUV quickly filled the gap between the two vehicles. The rain was coming down in sheets like a tropical storm. The windshield wipers flapped uselessly. The palms of Tony's hands began to sweat. His heart was pounding. The reflection in the rearview mirror of the two bright headlights hurt his eyes. He reached up to dim the reflector on the mirror.

Suddenly Tony felt a hard bump as the SUV rammed him from behind. He looked around trying to find a safe way off of the road, but all he could see was a slight gravel embankment, beyond which, large trees had been planted at intervals.

Again, the SUV bumped him from behind, this time accelerating in the process. Tony's old Volvo was no match for the powerful SUV. His car spun off the road to the right, speeding along the gravel embankment. Tony hit the breaks, only to skid forward on the gravel. He tried to steer the car back up onto the highway, but he could feel himself losing control.

"Oh, God," Tony said, knowing that something really bad was about to happen. He turned the front wheels into the skid. Suddenly, in front of him, he saw a huge oak tree.

As Tony's car hurtled toward the massive trunk of the oak tree, everything seemed to be happening in slow motion.

Certain that he was about to die, Tony cried out, "Cassandra... I love you."

At that moment, an enormous bolt of lightning struck a large maple tree that stood slightly to the right and in front of the oak tree. The lightning split the maple tree down the center, one half of the tree falling directly in the path of Tony's car, its heavily leaved branches acting as a leafy net, snaring Tony's Volvo, bringing it to a rough, but safe stop, inches from the massive trunk of the oak tree.

Tony, having passed out, was pinned back in his seat by the airbag that had deployed. The rain continued to pour down.

As if from afar, Tony heard a male voice ask, "Are you all right?"

Tony slowly started to regain consciousness. "Huh?"

"Are you all right, sir?" the male voice repeated.

Tony looked over and saw a man wearing the uniform of the New Jersey State Police, holding the car door open.

"I think so," Tony said, slowly beginning to grasp the fact that he was still alive.

"Try not to move," the trooper said. "We'll have you out of there in no time."

* * *

Cassandra was pacing back and forth in her room, trying to figure out how to reach Tony, when she heard his ring tone on her cell phone.

"Tony," she said, putting the phone to her ear. "Where are you?"

"I'm in the emergency room at the Bergen Regional Medical Center. I had an accident."

"Are you hurt?" she asked, her voice filled with alarm.

"I'm a little banged up, but I'm okay," Tony said. "The car's in pretty bad shape though."

"I don't care about the car," Cassandra said. "When will you be home?"

"Mom and Dad are on their way here now. Once I've been cleared, they'll take me back to the house. It'll probably be pretty late. Can I see you tomorrow?"

"Of course."

"You know, I've been thinking." Tony said. "The past few days have been kind of weird. First, the rock hits my windshield… then the sign falls off the roof at The Tavern… and now this. I could've sworn that that SUV was trying to run me off the road."

Cassandra was silent.

"Either I'm having a string of really bad luck," Tony said, "or someone has it in for me."

Chapter Twenty-Eight
THE VISITATION

Cassandra stood at her bedroom window, looking at the black sky. *If only I had called earlier*, she thought, angry at herself.

"Honey?" Maria said, standing in the doorway.

"Huh?" Cassandra turned around, startled by her mother's voice.

"Are you hungry?" Maria asked. "I could make you a quick sandwich."

"No, thanks."

"Dana said she'd call as soon as they get home."

"Okay. I think I'm going to lie down for a little while,"

Cassandra said.

"You know, it's a miracle that Tony survived the crash," Maria added. "The police said that he was headed straight for a big tree."

"How do you know that?" Cassandra asked.

"Dana told me. It was in the police report," Maria said, turning to leave. "I'll let you know when she calls."

"Thanks, Mom."

Maria headed downstairs for the kitchen.

Cassandra walked over to her bureau and opened the top drawer. Reaching inside, she withdrew the pouch containing the stone and the small box, which held the sprig from the lilac wreath. Placing both items on top of her bureau, she stood there for a moment, looking at them. Carefully lifting the top of the little box, she looked inside. The petals, now wilted and discolored had fallen to the bottom of the box. Cassandra then turned her attention to the pouch with the stone. Opening the pouch, she took out the stone. Walking over to her bed, she sat down, holding the stone in her right hand. She waited a moment. Nothing. Changing it to her left hand, she closed her eyes tightly and concentrated.

Cassandra started to feel a strange sensation. It was as though she was being pulled toward something, but here was nothing to be seen. There was only blackness... darker than night. Beginning to feel drowsy, she lay back on the bad, resting her head on the pillow. As she drifted off to sleep, she felt the stone drop out of her hand and fall to the carpet.

Suddenly, Cassandra awoke, sensing a presence in her room. Someone was standing at the foot of her bed. It took a few moments for Cassandra's vision to adjust to the semi-darkness. When it did, she was horrified to see a girl in a white dress, soaked with blood.

"It's me! Cassandra," the girl said. "I've come to say goodbye."

It took Cassandra a few seconds to realize that the bloody apparition before her was that of little Cassandra, no longer the little girl, but now, a young woman in her early twenties.

"I felt that you were trying to reach me," the apparition said, her voice shaky.

"Yes. I was trying to get back to Troy," Cassandra said.

"Troy is no longer," the dying Cassandra said. "Everything that you told me came to pass. The attack by the Greek army… the destruction of Troy. My entire family was killed."

"You're hurt," Cassandra said, looking at the blood stained dress.

"I'm dying."

"No, you can't," Cassandra said, tears starting to form in her eyes.

"Do not cry, little sister. I am about to join my family in the other world," the apparition said. "But first, there are some things that you have to know."

Cassandra stared at her.

"I have very little time left," the dying Cassandra continued. "When Apollo bestowed the gift of prophecy on me, I made an oath, promising him my love. When I chose another for my lover, he cursed me so that no one would believe me." She paused a moment. "Now that I am gone, Apollo will come for you. You must live up to your promise."

"What promise?" Cassandra asked.

"The promise of your love."

"I never made such a promise," Cassandra said.

"Then why is he after you?"

Cassandra thought for a moment, then said, "My father took an oath to Apollo during a ceremony before I was born."

"An oath cannot be broken," the apparition said.

"But it wasn't me who took the oath," Cassandra protested. "It was my father."

"But Apollo still wants *you*." The dying Cassandra paused for a moment, then continued. "There is something else that I must warn you of."

"What is it?" Cassandra asked.

"Is there someone that you love?"

"Yes."

"Beware! Your love is putting him in great danger. Apollo will destroy the one you love."

"What can I do?"

"In order to protect the life of the one you love, Apollo must never learn of your love."

"But how can I hide it?"

"You can't. Apollo will know if you love another and will destroy him. You must harden your heart. Let it be like a stone. Let no love shine through."

"I don't know if I can do that."

"Then you must learn how to. If you don't, the one you love is doomed."

The dying Cassandra coughed. A terrible rasping sound came from her lungs. "I must go now," she whispered, hoarsely. "There is no time left." The apparition of the dying Cassandra began to fade. "This is our last time together. Goodbye little sister." The apparition continued to fade.

"Don't go!" Cassandra called out, sitting up.

The apparition vanished completely.

Cassandra, no longer able to hold back the tears, cried openly, the tears streaming down her face.

~ Cassandra ~

Chapter Twenty-Nine

HEART OF STONE

Cassandra awoke slowly, forgetting for a moment the events of the night before. She looked over at the window. The rain was coming down steadily. Throwing back the covers, she sat up, swinging her legs over the side of the bed.

As Cassandra stood up, she felt something under her left foot. *The stone!* The events of the night before came rushing back to her... the visit of the dying Cassandra and her warning... *'You must harden your heart. Let it be like a stone.'*

Cassandra reached down and picked up the stone.

Walking over to her bureau, she put the stone in its pouch and pulled the drawstring tight. She looked at the little box containing the withered sprig. Putting the lid on it, she opened the top drawer of the bureau and put both the pouch and the box in the drawer.

Glancing at herself in the mirror, Cassandra noticed that she was still wearing the gold heart that Tony had given her. Quickly undoing the clasp on the chain, she took off the necklace and put it in the drawer. *I can't let my feelings show*, she thought, as she pushed the drawer shut.

Walking over to her desk, Cassandra lifted her cell phone out of its charging cradle. There were seven messages from Tony.

"Honey?" Maria called up from the kitchen. "Is your phone turned off? Tony's been trying to reach you. He just called again."

"Tell him I'm not feeling well," Cassandra called back. She could hear Maria climbing the stairs.

"What's the matter, honey?" Maria asked, standing in the doorway of Cassandra's room.

"I just don't feel like seeing him."

Maria stood still, a confused look on her face. "Did you two have an argument?"

"No," Cassandra said, looking a little annoyed. "Just tell him I'm not feeling well, okay?"

"Alright, honey," Maria replied, heading back downstairs.

The phone in the kitchen rang. Maria answered it, spoke for about a minute, then hung up the receiver. "That was Tony," she called up to Cassandra. "He wants to see you. He sounded pretty determined. He said he'll be here in a few minutes."

Cassandra did not respond.

* * *

A few moments later, the front doorbell rang. Opening the door, Cassandra saw Tony, half-soaked from the rain, standing on the porch holding a small bunch of flowers in his outstretched hand.

"These are for you," he said, smiling.

"Why are you *doing* this?" she asked, a coldness in her voice. She couldn't help but notice the black and blue marks all over his face, visual signs of the accident of the previous day. *That's because of me*, she thought to herself.

"Your mom said you weren't feeling well. I thought these might cheer you up." He started to hand her the flowers.

"I don't want them," Cassandra said, coolly. "You just don't get it, do you?"

"Get what?" Tony asked, sensing that something was very wrong.

"That I don't want to see you," Cassandra said, surprised that she was able to get the words out.

"I can come back later," he said.

"No, Tony. I don't want you to come back."

Tony looked at her, the smile on his face gone. "What are you talking about?"

Seeing the pain on Tony's face, Cassandra felt herself weaken. Then she remembered the dying Cassandra's words, *'Harden your heart. Let it be like a stone.'*

"You heard me," Cassandra continued. "I don't want

to see you anymore."

Tony stared at her, unable to speak. He noticed that Cassandra was not wearing the gold heart that he had given her. "What did I do?" he asked, bewildered.

Unable to bear the sight of Tony's pain, Cassandra felt herself begin to weaken again. *Oh, God, I can't go through with this.* The words of the dying Cassandra came back to her. *"Apollo will destroy the one you love."*

Cassandra dug her fingernails into the palms of her hands in an effort to distract herself from the knowledge of the emotional pain that she was putting Tony through.

"Ow," she yelped, as one of her nails pierced her palm.

"What happened?" Tony asked, alarmed, seeing the blood.

"Go away!" Cassandra commanded, on the verge of tears. "Just go away."

Tony stood, numbly staring at her. "What did I *do*?" he asked, trying to fight back the tears that were stinging at his eyes. "You've got to tell me what I did wrong."

"Just go away, Tony."

"But I love you," he said.

Cassandra felt as if her heart were about to break.

"I thought you felt the same way about me," Tony said.

"You were wrong," Cassandra said. "I feel nothing for you."

Tony stared at her one more time, then turned and walked out into the rain.

Chapter Thirty

FOOTPRINTS IN THE SAND

Tony stood watching the waves as they crashed down upon the sandy shoreline. The rain had stopped, but the sky was still dark. Leaning against the wooden railing of the recently repaired wooden deck of The Tavern, he tried to relive the events of only two nights earlier. He thought back to when he and Cassandra had kissed and held each other so closely.

What did I do wrong? Tony asked himself. *Did I scare her away by telling her that I loved her?*

In his mind, Tony went over the last two days. He just couldn't figure it out. He had never seen Cassandra so cold and detached as when she told him that she didn't want to see him again. He recalled the last words she'd said to him. *'I feel nothing for you.'* Once again, the words went through him like a dagger. He felt a pain in his heart that he didn't know could exist.

Tony lowered his gaze for a moment. Out of the corner of his eye, he noticed a seagull, which had landed on the wooden railing a few feet from where he was standing. The seagull had something in its beak. Waddling over to Tony, the bird released a small round stone, placing it on the railing next to Tony.

Tony looked at the stone. Then he looked at the seagull. "Get out of here," he said, annoyed, waiving his hand at the seagull. Easily sidestepping Tony's hand, the bird walked back over to the stone, pushing it closer to Tony. "Go on. Get out of here," Tony yelled, angrily. The seagull, cocking its head to one side, looked up at Tony, then flew away.

Tony looked back out at the waves, watching them crash against the shore. He thought how easy it would be to just swim out as far he could, until he could swim no more, then simply sink to the bottom, ending his pain forever.

I can't do that to Mom and Dad, he thought to himself, imagining the pain he'd be causing them. But, then again, the thought of living without Cassandra was unbearable. Walking down the wooden steps to the sand, Tony stepped out of his loafers. The sand was cold and wet under his feet, but he didn't feel a thing. He began walking toward the promontory, which was at the far end of the beach, out of view of The Tavern.

* * *

"Maria, it's Dana," the voice on the phone said. "Is Tony there?"

"He left about an hour ago," Maria said.

"Is Cassandra with him?" Dana asked.

"No. She's upstairs," Maria replied. "Why?"

"My car's gone," Dana continued. "It's not like Tony to do that. He's never taken my car without asking me first." She paused for a moment. "Maria, do me a favor. Please ask Cassandra if she's spoken to Tony. Maybe she knows where he is."

Still holding the phone, Maria walked to the foot of the stairs. "Honey, have you spoken with Tony?"

Cassandra, staring out her bedroom window, did not respond.

"Honey," Maria repeated. "Dana's on the phone. She can't reach Tony. He's been gone for over an hour."

"I don't think she can hear me," Maria said into the phone. "I'll call you back as soon as I find out."

"Okay, thanks," Dana said, ending the call.

* * *

Maria stood in the doorway to Cassandra's room. She saw Cassandra standing at the window, staring out at the darkening sky.

"Honey?" Maria asked. "Dana wants to know if you've spoken with Tony. He's taken her car and she doesn't know where he's gone."

Cassandra turned to face her mother. Maria noticed that her daughter's face was puffy, her eyes red from crying.

"What's the matter?" Maria asked, alarmed. "Did you and Tony have an argument?"

"We broke up," Cassandra responded, trying to sound dispassionate.

"Oh, no!" Maria gasped. "What for?"

"I can't explain now," Cassandra said.

"Should I tell Dana?"

"No. Not yet," Cassandra said. Pausing a moment, she continued, "Mom, I need to be alone for a minute."

"Of course, honey," Maria said. She turned and headed back downstairs.

Tony's missing... it's my fault, Cassandra thought. *What if something happens to him? What if he tries to hurt himself? I'd die.*

Walking over to her bureau, she opened the top drawer, and retrieved the gold necklace that Tony had given her. As she picked it up, the little see-through charm with the lilac petal slid off the chain and fell into the drawer. Cassandra decided to leave it there. Looking in the mirror, she put the necklace with Tony's gold heart on it around her neck and attached the clasp.

Clutching the tiny gold heart in her hand, Cassandra closed her eyes, concentrating hard. At first she felt nothing. Then, suddenly, she felt the sensation of cold, wet sand under her feet. She concentrated harder. An image was beginning to form. Blurry at first, it started to come into focus.

Suddenly, Cassandra saw Tony walking on the wet sand toward the water.

"No, Tony! Don't!" she screamed.

Letting go of the gold heart, Cassandra grabbed her cell phone and quickly dialed Tony's number.

"Hi, this is Tony. I can't take your call..." Cassandra ended the call and ran downstairs.

"Mom, I know where Tony is," Cassandra said, breathless.

"Where?" Maria asked.

"The Tavern," Cassandra said. "Come on. We've got to hurry."

*　　*　　*

"Hurry, Mom. Faster," Cassandra urged Maria.

"I'm already going more than the speed limit," Maria said, glancing down at the speedometer, then up at the rearview mirror.

Moments later, Maria turned off the highway and into the parking lot of The Tavern.

"There it is!" Cassandra said, immediately recognizing Dana's car parked by one of the light poles. She started to open her door before Maria even had a chance to stop the car.

"Should I wait?" Maria asked, pulling into a parking space.

"No. I'll be alright. You go on home," Cassandra said, getting out of the car and closing the door. She ran across the parking lot and around to the back of The Tavern.

"Please let him be there," Cassandra said to herself.

Running up the sand-covered wooden steps that led to the deck, Cassandra saw a janitor sweeping away the sand that had blown onto the deck during the storm.

"Have you seen a guy about this tall?" Cassandra

asked, holding her hand above her head. "He was wearing a white polo shirt and khaki chinos."

"I saw him about twenty minutes ago," the janitor said. He pointed toward the promontory. "It looked like he was headed out to the point."

Cassandra hurried down the back steps of the deck. Her heart sank at the sight of Tony's loafers, placed neatly, side by side, in the sand. She looked down the beach in the direction that the janitor had been pointing. There was no sign of Tony.

Oh, God, she prayed silently. *Please don't let me be too late.*

Suddenly she noticed footprints in the wet sand. She started running, following them. The footprints led down the beach to a curve in the shoreline beyond which Cassandra could not see.

A light rain had begun to fall. The wind was blowing in her face.

"Tony!" she yelled.

Cassandra continued to run along the shoreline, which curved around, leading toward the promontory. All of a sudden, the footprints disappeared, having been washed away by the fast incoming tide. She continued running toward the rocky promontory.

"Tony!" she called out again, her voice muffled by the wind and rain.

* * *

Tony looked down at the foamy surf crashing onto the rocks on which he was standing. His bare feet were bleeding, cut from having climbed across the sharp rocks. He thought he heard his name being called in the wind. *That sounds like Cassandra,* Tony thought. *I must be hallucinating.*

The sky was growing darker by the minute. The rain was coming down harder now. Thunder rumbled in the distance.

*　*　*

No longer trying to hide her love, Cassandra ran faster. Soaked from the rain and out of breath, she prayed, "Oh, God, please let him be alive."

An enormous bolt of lightning flashed across the sky. In the distance, illuminated by the lightning, Cassandra saw Tony standing at the end of the rocky promontory, the waves crashing violently around him.

"Tony!" she yelled, as loud as she could.

Suddenly, tripping on a piece of driftwood, Cassandra fell onto the hard wet sand.

Another bolt of lightning lit up the sky. Raising her head, Cassandra looked at the rocky promontory where Tony had been standing. He was gone!

"No-o-o-o!" she screamed.

The waves were now crashing onto the promontory with a fury. Cassandra struggled to get up, but she couldn't move her feet. Looking down, she saw that a large clump of seaweed had wrapped itself around her ankles. Out of frustration and anger at herself, she began to cry.

I let him down. He was always there for me, she thought. *This was the one time he needed me... and I wasn't there for him.*

The tide was coming in faster now. A wave rolled onto the beach, splashing up against Cassandra. She could taste the salt water in her mouth. *I'm going to die, too.*

The thought of dying didn't frighten her, as she couldn't imagine life without Tony.

At that moment, she felt someone lifting her up off the wet sand. She looked up. It was Tony! She couldn't believe her eyes.

"I thought you were dead," she said.

Bending down, he removed the seaweed that was wrapped around her ankles. "I saw you fall," he said, helping her to her feet.

"How can you even think of helping me after all those horrible things I said to you this morning?" Cassandra asked, her eyes filling with tears.

"Did you mean them?" he asked, a questioning look on his face.

"No."

"Then why did you say them?"

"To protect you," she said.

"Protect me?" Tony asked. "From what?"

"Last night, I used the stone again," Cassandra said.

Tony flashed back momentarily to the seagull and the stone that it had kept trying to push toward him. *It was trying to tell me...*

"I was holding it in my hand and fell asleep." She paused for a moment, then continued. "Cassandra came to me, but she was no longer a little girl. She was older than me and her dress was all bloody. She had just been stabbed and was dying. It was horrible."

Tony looked at her, trying to take in what she was saying. "What does that have to do with me?"

"She warned me that Apollo would destroy anyone that

I loved."

"And that's why you said what you did… that you felt nothing for me?"

"Yes. I wanted Apollo to think that I didn't love you."

"Well, it worked," Tony said. "*I* believed you. I wanted to die."

"Oh, Tony…" Cassandra started to say, finding it difficult to speak through her tears. Looking up at Tony, she noticed that he had been crying, too.

"I'll fight for you," Tony said. "I'm not afraid of Apollo."

"I'll fight *with* you," Cassandra said.

At that moment, a large wave rolled onto the beach, stopping only inches from where they were standing.

Putting their arms around one another, they held each other for a long moment.

"I love you, Tony," Cassandra said.

"I love you, too," Tony said.

Pulling slightly away, Cassandra looked up at him.

Tony gently touched his lips to hers, rain and salt water mixing with their tears as they kissed.

A sudden bolt of lightning flashed across the sky, followed by a loud, angry crack of thunder.

"Come on," Tony said. "Let's go home."

Holding tightly onto one another, Tony and Cassandra walked back down the beach toward The Tavern.

High above them, unobserved, a lone seagull circled once, then slowly flew away.

End of Book Two

Coming next

The Journey

~SP~
Studio Publishing

Be sure to follow *CASSANDRA*
on Twitter:

@CASSANDRA_novel

And visit our website:

www.studiopublishing.net

~SP~
Studio Publishing